Tales from the Featherbed

*for
Kerry

Bill Smith
Jan. 20, 96*

Bill Smith's
Tales from the Featherbed

Edited by
Vaughn Ramsey Ward

Bowman Books
Greenfield Review Press
Greenfield Center, New York

ISBN 0–912678–91–7
LIBRARY OF CONGRESS #94–75712

FIRST EDITION
Bowman Books #7
Bowman Books is an imprint of The Greenfield
Review Press. All of the volumes in this series
are devoted to the contemporary tellings of
traditional tales.

Design and composition by Sans Serif
Typesetters, Ann Arbor, Michigan

Distributed by The Talman Co. Inc.
131 Spring Street
New York, N.Y. 10012
(212) 431–7175   Fax (212) 431–7215

ADIRONDACK MEMORIES

Oh those beautiful hills, they hold memories for me,
Those beautiful Adirondack hills,
Where the grass is so green and the air is so clear,
And at night you can hear the whippoorwills.

Those beautiful hills where the trout jump for flies,
And the trees stand so straight and so tall
On the side of a hill overlooking a stream
Is the most lovely place of them all.

There stands our old home, it's now silent and still
Though our laughter still flows on the breeze
And there's a large clump of sumac where the barn
    used to stand
And the meadows they have all grown to trees.

Now this is the place where us children were born,
And our Ma and our Pa worked so hard.
For we lived off the land from the fish and the deer
And the gardens that were in our backyard.

Now we had a small farm that we worked everyday
But it scarcely would pay for the cows.
And we raised our own pigs and our chickens and our
    geese
And the horses they were good with the plow.

I can still see my mother with her hair silver white
As she worked around that old kitchen stove.
Baking pies for us kids from the berries we had picked
In the shade on the side of a knoll.

Now us kids would walk to school whether sun or rain
  or snow,
'Bout a mile and a half down the road.
And when school was let out we hurried home to do
  our chores,
For we all had to carry our load.

When the work was done at night we carried water
  from the well,
And that old washing tub we would fill.
And we'd all take our baths and get reminded of our
  prayers,
Then Ma would send us up the wooden hill.

As I sit and reminisce about our old country home
And these memories come to me at will,
I have to thank God for all the good times we have had
In those beautiful Adirondack hills.

Oh those beautiful hills, they hold memories for me,
Those beautiful Adirondack hills,
Where the grass is so green and the air is so clear,
And at night you can hear the whippoorwills.

—Words and music by Bill Smith—

To my parents,

Roy Smith and Emily Bicknell Smith,

and my brothers and sisters,

Cassie, Kenneth, Frank, Durwood,
Roswell, Bernice, Betty, Richard and Sady.

CONTENTS

JUST THINGS HE PICKED UP
[While Everyone Else Was Putting Them Down!]

All them old timers would go up there
and spit into the ash bucket
and the round oak stove
and drink "sody pop," as they called it.

They'd tell stories and lie.
What a time they'd have!

So I took these guys
and stuck them into these stories.

The stories aren't necessarily true,
but the people and the background and the atmosphere
—that's all true.

—Bill Smith—

Last May I drove out of our Eastern Mohawk Valley canal village, up past Lake George, and northwest into the Central Adirondacks. Finally, in Long Lake (when I found a place that was open year round), I bought a map—which told me I was only half-way there. An hour and a half later, west of Tupper Lake, the country . . . well, I can't say it flattened out, exactly. It was more like an unfolding: darkly-forested foothills, wider valleys, small, scattered settlements not quite so green as our Eastern slopes, where something grey-green [lichen?] crusted the plateau-like rocks.[1]

I had made it to St. Lawrence County's *Featherbed*, on the Western Adirondack slopes near Ontario, Canada, the Mohawk reservation, and the St. Lawrence Seaway. The Featherbed, a place where the past still extends well beyond one's own lifespan, has been home to several generations of Bill Smith's woods farm family.

"Not far now," I told myself. I had Sal Smith's promised venison supper and some good talk on my mind.

Two more turns off the main road and there they were—next door to the house where Bill grew up after his family moved down from the Featherbed, where the Law brothers had the kitchen hops Bill had told me about. There was Bill's basket and trapping cabin on the right surrounded by the most magnificent mountain flower gardens I've ever seen. By the time I was inside, I realized that Bill and Sal made their house as they have their lives: together and with their own hands.

I had come to record the stories for this book. The next day, Bill talked and I taped. They took me up to the Featherbed after supper. Up a long farm lane, past the old spring house on the left by the brook, before the clapboard center hall farmhouse, Bill pointed out the remains of the stone wall where his older brothers and sisters took that big spill. I saw where Ira Irish and the others lived, marveling at Bill's gift in bringing back a whole generation of people and stories, some gone before Bill was born.

The way of life is not gone. The Featherbed is far enough from big population centers that people born before 1945 grew up in an *oral*, rather than a *print*, or *media* culture, in a world that relished talk.[2] Bill was the only small child at home. Born to parents in their forties with nine much older brothers and sisters, Bill soaked in his elders' talk without distractions from age-mates. Like an only child, he made up for his loneliness with imagination:

> *I remember back when I was three or four years old. I remember playing out in the yard. And I remember that all my brothers and sisters were grown up and gone. I made up brothers and sisters and used to talk to them. One day my brother that was next to me caught me talking to these make-believe people. He really gave me a hard*

time. I was real embarrassed about it, but it didn't stop me. I still did it because they were important to me.

The North Country is known for its guide-raconteurs and its live-in lumber camps. The extreme cold, the practical jokes, the enormous quantities of food, the fights, the woods skills—true and stretched—make up a large body of oral literature as well as the model for an American stage and fiction stereotype: the Yankee backwoodsman.[3] Most traditional Adirondack stories feature the isolated man's world of woods work, hunting, and fishing. *Tales from the Featherbed* tells us, finally, what went on at home while the men were in the woods all winter. If Bill's family was at all typical, Mother could do—and wasn't afraid of—anything.

Even the littlest child worked. Bill learned by watching and doing.

Here's a list of stuff I grew up knowing how to do. I grew up knowing how to milk cows and how to take care of animals . . . certain remedies. Anything that worked for a horse, they'd use it on a kid. We used to drink the Watkins Liniment, take turpentine and sugar once a month for worms and, if you didn't have turpentine, a teaspoon of kerosene would do the same thing. We learned how to rid a horse of colic and be up half the night feeding them Epsom Salts and water and cleaning them out with your sleeves rolled up and all that business.

So you learned a little bit about how to work a horse and how to harness a horse and how to work in a hay field and how to cut wood with a crosscut saw and split wood and pile it so that the rain didn't get in it. There was all kinds of little tricks to everything, little country things that country folks learned about.

The family didn't have electricity until 1954, when Bill was seventeen. People came in at night to sing songs and tell stories, much as they had done at the place on the Featherbed where they lived until Bill was five:

> . . . Up at the old Featherbed my mother had a big round oak stove that set in the front parlor. That was the stage setting, sort of. Whoever was doing their piece at that time would be standing there or sitting by the round oak stove, whichever they preferred.
> The stairway was sort of the gallery. It went up and veered off to the left and went upstairs. And people would be sitting all down the stairway. Whenever somebody got through, why, they'd take their place in the stairway and somebody else would get up there and do a little piece. That was wintertime stuff. In the warm time, why you'd sit on the back porch.
> This happened once a week, on the weekends, and then more. We did it ourselves; we entertained. When I was a kid I used to entertain, too. I could sing songs. My mother loved to sing. She never was without a tune in her mind and I'm the same way. There's always a tune. I might be doing something else, or she might be doing something else, but in her mind she was accompanying all of this with a song or with a tune or a poem.

Old stories—ridiculing laziness, untested "book learning," and putting on airs—taught kids what the community expected: hard work, common sense, modesty and adaptability. No matter how many times and how many ways circumstances knocked you down, if the cows needed milking, you simply got up one more time and milked those cows.[4] City slickers were fair game.[5]

After Bill got his first guitar and learned a few chords the local fiddlers took an interest in him.

> . . . . A kid ain't long pickin' that stuff up, especially if they're telling you how great you are. . . . I was becoming a big shot right then and there. It was just all kinds of fun for me getting all this attention. Stanley Carey used to be one of the fiddlers around all these kitchen hops and bars and stuff. . . . Then I got mixed up with some other fiddlers and I'd go to Cook's Corners and play. That's where I got so well acquainted with all those great Cook's Corners people.

My sister used to run the general store over there. On Friday and Saturday nights they came down out of the hills like little soldiers—all coming down to the general store. Old Austin Burdick would bring his banjo and his fiddle and sit around there and play. Lanty Martin would be back and forth with his hounds. And then there was people like Earl Phillips.

The family memory goes back from Canada to France, Scotland and England. Peter Smith, Bill's grandfather, was a red-haired Scotsman from Ontario. Grandmother Smith was French and Indian. His mother's family, the Bicknells, Bill thinks, were Scots and English. They all farmed and worked in the woods.

My Grandmother Bicknell had my mother and my Uncle John. Grandma and Grandpa Bicknell would work in the logging camps and my mother used to go from one camp to the other. In the winter time she used to board out somewhere and go to school.

My mother's mother was married twice. She was married to a fellow by the name of MacDonald first. . . . They had a son and a daughter. The daughter got killed somehow running around and got her neck caught in a clothesline. Uncle Jim used to play the fiddle and the mouth organ and the spoons and step dance all the time. He was a lot of fun to be around. Parted his hair in the middle and he was a character. He was my mother's half brother.

Grandma, at that time MacDonald, heard the whistle blow at the mill. Whenever someone got hurt at the mill, they blew the whistle so you knew that there was an accident. It wasn't long until somebody came to the door. Her husband had been working on or near one of the saws and a tailing come off the saw and speared him straight through. She later married Bicknell. I guess he was a good enough guy, but he had a terrible drinking problem. And I think that's why my mother hated drinking so much.

They were poor, Bill is fond of saying, as far as money went, but they were rich in other ways.

We had all we wanted to eat with gardens and pigs and chickens, milk and butter from the farm and fish and deer from the woods. And we had plenty of love. We'd go to school barefoot, patches on our pants. My mother always said it didn't matter if you had patches on your clothes as long as the clothes were clean. You were clean and you was a good person. It didn't make no difference if you had patches on your pants or not.

It wasn't easy when they moved from the one room country school to the village school in Colton.[6]

When the school centralized, they sent all us kids who had gone to country schools here into the village school. Nobody particularly wanted it. All these strangers show up. We might have only been from three miles away but we were considered as outsiders. When we got to school we got made fun of and we'd get in fights. Of course, we'd finish 'em because we worked every day and we were strong kids. Those kids weren't strong—only in the mouth! And once they got slapped, they were out of business. They would run in to the teacher and of course she'd snake us in by the ear and fling us in the corner and stick a dunce hat on us. So the relationship with that school stunk as far as I was concerned.

Bill says many kids from the country left school because of that treatment. Called "hillbillies," even by some teachers, the country kids were ridiculed because of their bran and flour sack shirts and blouses. The *homemade bread* was a target because it made their sandwiches too thick. Some kids, Bill says, wouldn't eat lunch. It was easier to go hungry than to be hurt one more time. The bus driver, Bill Sanford, laughed when they got on the bus, saying, "Here come those Pancake Kids. You can always tell because you smell just like pancakes." All because they were part of a traditional culture. Prejudice and cruelty have a price: Smart boys from Bill's neighborhood saw themselves as dunces and gave up.

Bill's brother, Richard, had a hard time with the school in town. He left school when he was sixteen to work in the woods for a winter before joining the Merchant Marine.

He spent all them months on the ocean and he read all that time and he went to all these foreign countries and when he came back from the Merchant Marines he was very well-educated, a very smart man. . . . There isn't anything that man doesn't know about. And he learned it all from books.

But if they'd a gave him a chance in school he'd a been smart there, too.

Frank got by in school by wearing the clown's mask.

Frank acted like he didn't have both oars in the water. He was so busy being comical that people didn't think he was smart. But he was smart. You couldn't get five words out of him without getting something comical, and so everybody just thought he was sort of a clown-type. I think that hurt him in a way because people didn't ever take him serious. But he's certainly nobody's fool.

People think I'm funny but that man was fifty times funnier than I am.

When Bill was sixteen, he quit school, too. His mother got him his first job at Harry Ford's sawmill.

Her and Harry thought if he worked me hard enough I would go back to school, so he put me to piling wood in the mill yard. It was hot out there, but I had piled wood since I was a baby and I did not want to pile wood. I wanted to work in the mill or pile lumber or something like that, but I did not want to pile wood. So I didn't. Harry told my Mother he had to let me go, which was fine with me. I got my own job at the golf course in Potsdam.

Bill hitchhiked to work in Potsdam for two years. He also cut pulpwood in the spring, trapped in the fall and put in some time playing music in the local bars—all before he turned 18.

'Course I wasn't supposed to play in the bars, but I did. At that time there was illegal bars around where it didn't make no difference if you had pink working papers or not because they weren't supposed to have the bar there in the first place. There was a lot of these different places. There was an old fellow—Honey Cadew, we called him—his last name was MacDonald and he had a still in his cellar up there. And old Honey Cadew had goats. He used to let the goats in the house all the time.

According to local gossip, one day Honey was messing with his still down cellar and—I always wondered—folks never knew whether a goat did it or what happened, but something got tipped over and the still blew up and burnt the house and burnt old Honey and the goats right up. And that was the end of the liquor business.

But we used to play at those things and on Saturday nights the place was just packed with people. They'd come there and dance and have a time.

Sal moved next door in 1953. Bill and Sal got married in 1955, when Bill was 18. That next fall, when golfing season was over, Bill moved houses from the soon-to-be-flooded St. Lawrence Valley. For a number of years he alternated working on the seaway, working construction, trapping and cutting pulp wood. He even worked for three years as a milkman. Finally, Bill says he " . . . got fed up with the construction business and got into the trapping business."

I grew up around trappers and hunters and guides and all that. . . . Eddie Surrey was a trapper. I knew how to make lures . . . there was this wonderful old trapper, old fellow called E.J. Daley that taught me a lot. He run a trapping supply business. He died in the '60's. Before he died he told me all kinds of things: different recipes for making lures and different types of things. So I was well-equipped when the time come that I wanted to do that.

Somewhere in the mid 1970's, Bill started making baskets. Many Mohawk people who worked in the woods stayed at Bill's parents' in the summer and made baskets. They taught Bill.

The basket-making comes from that because I grew up around basket makers. So all these are just things I picked up. One day, in my early 30's my trapping baskets were falling apart.

I said to Sal, "I don't know why I'm buying those baskets. They're split too thin. The material isn't any good. I could make them when I was a kid."

Sal said, "Why, you don't know how to do that!"

So I went out and cut an ash tree and beat it with a head ax and got some splints and started making baskets. People saw them and I've been doing it ever since.

Bill added Adirondack furniture and snowshoes to the trapping and basket-making. With characteristic energy and canniness, he developed his skills into a lecture and guiding service for the near-by colleges [St. Lawrence University, the State University of New York at Potsdam, SUNY Canton, and Clarkson].

. . . then I put an ad in the colleges that I was a guide and that I would take college professors and students out into the mountains, take them hiking or canoeing . . . and next thing I knew I was getting calls. The professors would come. Of course, with the trapping things, I had all these animal carcasses and whatever for the biology people to check out. Well, they were going wild over these things. . . . And the next thing I knew they had me in the colleges giving lectures on outdoors and basket making and survival in the wilderness—trees and edibles and non-edibles and all kinds of woodsy things.

In 1976, Bill worked in Canton, New York, as history teacher Charlie Franklin's aide. At the same time, Bill took college courses, bought fur from trappers and made baskets. Charlie died, and Bill left Canton for a teachers' assistant job at Parrishville School. He finished a degree in Outdoor Education. Bill got three New York State Board of Regents' Awards for the outdoor education program he started in Parrishville. And then, like most dedicated teachers, Bill " . . . burned out on high school boys."

Bill remembers the first time, around 1980 or 1981, he officially told stories in public:

> *Marnie Crowell, she was one of the college people that used to come here, her and her husband Ken. She got me to go and do stories by kind of fibbing to me. She called one day and said, "How would you like to come to the storytelling festival?"*
>
> *I got there and Varrick Chittenden was waiting at the door for me, and he said, "Come on in. Marnie's down at the fireside lounge waiting for you."*
>
> *So I went down and there was Marnie sitting there up front with an empty chair sitting next to her chair. She stood up and said, "Here's our guest speaker now."*
>
> *And I said, "You've got to be nuts. . . . I'm not telling stories!"*
>
> *"Well," she said, "I knew you wouldn't if I asked you to come, so I tricked you into it. I just want you to tell them some of the stories that you tell me around the campfire up home."*
>
> *So I did. And that was the beginning of storytelling.*

* * * * *

When Bill got going, my own rural, war-time childhood came back. *The Eyes and Ears of the World* newsreel changed once a week at the theater in town. Kids got in for a nickel. That's where we all learned to read our first words, the same two words for every one of us who read before we went to school—*bomb* and *war*. And all the time, (weirdly), one day to the next, things for children went on pretty much as they always had. Outhouses, kerosene lamps, the pump in the kitchen or by the back door, patchwork quilts, heavy comforters pieced from wool scraps, everything from underwear to dresses and shirts made from cotton flour sacks, were as taken for granted as the black-out window shades. Mules and draft horses pulled the plows that turned the furrows. Cellar shelves crazy-quilted with big green and yellow and red glass jars—canned bounty from the Victory Garden and the hunt. Even people in town kept chickens.

Bill Smith, who has become New York State's best-known traditional storyteller, restores our collective memory, bringing back the last minute before tract housing and centralized schools, before the mobility of the GI Bill cut us off at the roots—a time when people "went visiting," children "knew their place," and elders had stories to tell. His kid's-eye view of World War II in rural St. Lawrence County blends autobiography with the tallest of Smith's trademark tales so deftly we're not always certain which is which.

After the war, young people were urged to "better themselves"—in other words, to pull up, and to deny, their roots. Most of our generation of country kids couldn't wait to get away, to take on an overlay of citification. Bill stayed right there by the Featherbed, building a life in the place and with the tools his tradition gave him. While everyone else seemed to be getting rid of the old furniture and the old ways, Bill and Sal Smith brought up their kids next door to the house where Bill's family was living when Sal's family moved in on the other side.

Bill and Sal's grandchildren are the fourth St. Lawrence County-born Smith generation. Their son Joe, a corrections officer, lives on adjoining land. Their daughters, Carol Smith Ferguson and the twins, Laurie Smith LaForce and Linda Bogart, live in and around Ogdensburg—close enough for Sal to meet them for lunch and Bill to help when things need fixing. Joe carries on the basket making. Bill isn't sure anyone in his family is likely to carry on the storytelling tradition.

I had been sitting, curled up on the couch in their tidy living room, for five hours! Now and then Bill had gotten up from his chair in the corner, to illustrate a point with a wide arm sweep, or a particular stance, or Lanty Martin's sideways walk. But mostly we'd been living in that other, vertical, memory time, unaware of clock time and the creeping stiffness in our fifty-something joints. We stretched, got a cup of coffee, smelled Sal's supper.

We sipped our coffee-looking out the new glassed-in side porch's perfectly clean windows at color-coordinated flower beds, blossoming trees, and bird feeders. We eased back to May 1993.

"What," I asked him, " would you do differently if you had a chance?"

I was kind of cocky when I was young and sort of belligerent. Had a kind of a chip on my shoulder. That's one thing I wouldn't do. . . .

It's the school of hard knocks. I've worked hard and I've worked around a lot of hard people, so I learned a lot.

I've helped a lot of young people . . . and I want that to continue.

Bill's glad his stories give people something they seem to need.

I just feel like I'm invitin' people to sit with me on my side porch while I tell 'em how it was.

What does he want people to remember about Bill Smith?

. . . . that I was good to them somewhere along the way.

Vaughn Ramsey Ward
Rexford, New York
Spring 1994

NOTES

[1]*Robert D. Bethke.* Adirondack Voices: Woodsmen and Woods Lore. *[Chicago: University of Illinois Press, 1981]. Bethke recorded the songs and stories of Northern St. Lawrence County woodsmen who were elderly in the early 1970's.* Adirondack Voices, *a scholarly work for the general reader, is a must for the serious student of Adirondack culture. Two books of fine first-person reminiscences by Western Adirondack foothills woodsmen are Herbert H.* Keith, Man of the Woods *[introduction and notes by Paul F. Jamieson Syracuse: Syracuse University Press, 1972] and Ray Hanlon, ed.,* A Man from the Past *[Big Moose, N.Y.: Big Moose Press, 1974].*

[2]*George Ewart Evans,* Where Beards Wag All: The Relevance of the Oral Tradition. *[London: Faber and Faber, Ltd., 1970]. Evans' study of the rural work culture of an East Anglian village focuses on the "oral testimony of those who grew up under the old culture, . . . giving voice to a class of people who otherwise had little chance to speak for themselves."*

[3]*Constance Rourke,* American Humor: A Study of the National Character. *[New York: Harcourt, Brace Jonavich, 1931. Reprint with introduction and bibliographic essay by W.T. Lhamon, Jr., Tallahassee: University of Florida, 1986]. Rourke traces jokes about the city traveller defeated by sharp and uncouth rural folk from the Yorkshire man in early English folk drama and to the "Jonathan Slick in New York" stage skits popular in the 1830's.*

[4]*Robert Corrigan, "The Comic Spirit," in* Comedy: Meaning and Form. *Robert Corrigan, ed. [Scranton, Pa.: Chandler Publishing Company, 1965]. "The constant in comedy is the comic view of life: the sense that no matter how many times man is knocked down he . . . manages to pull himself up and keep on going."*

[5]*Rourke.* American Humor.

[6]*Daniella Gioseffi, ed.* On Prejudice: A Global Perspective, *introduction by Daniella Gioseffi. [New York: Doubleday Anchor, 1993]. An anthology of acclaimed writers from around the globe addressing the many faces of projection, stereotyping, and scapegoating.* Part Two: Cultural Destruction and Cultural Affirmation *examines, among other issues,* social class discrimination.

ROY SMITH'S BOY

If one exists as a human being,
he must be hypersensitive to the absurd;
and the most absurd contradiction of all
is . . . having to live amid the irrational,
the ludicrous, the disgusting, or the perilous.

—Wylie Sypher—

The best tall tales are only improvements on reality.

—Jan Harold Brunvand—

STRONGEST MAN IN THE NORTH COUNTRY

When my father was a little boy, he was with his father, my grandfather. My grandfather's name was Peter Smith, a great mammoth Scotsman. He looked like a giant Yosemite Sam. He had fire red whiskers and a huge red mustache that curled way out. His face was like a foot and a half wide. He was a big brute. My Grandfather Smith was a huge brute of a man. When I was a kid, every time you'd be out working with your father in the fields or there was something and you couldn't lift, or you're trying to roll a big rock out and you couldn't roll the rock out, my father would say,

"Good thing your grandfather can't see you. He was the strongest man in the North Country you know."

"Yes, Dad, I know, you've told me this before."

"And you knew that his wrist was six inches wide, didn't you?"

And I'd say, "Yeah, you told me that, too."

And he'd say, "Did I ever tell you about the time," (and none of these old fellers ever said *Italian*, they always said *Eye-talian*) "Did I ever tell you about the time that the Eyetalians were down on the back Hanawah Road? Now them Eyetalian fellers were brought here to cut and carve Potsdam Sandstone and make the monuments and all these big sandstone buildings that you see around Potsdam. Beautiful, beautiful work."

Peter and my father, who was just a little guy sitting on the seat of the wagon, had been down to the grain store to get a load of grain for the horses. They had that big lumber wagon loaded with grain heading for somewhere with it, either to the woods or to his house or wherever he kept his horses.

These fellers had one of them big monuments

3

they had just made, gone through the bottom of one of them wagons. They had to get the other wagon off it and get it off to one side and get another wagon up there. It was just taking forever. Grampa Smith didn't have any patience at all. None whatsoever. And he's sittin' there gettin' fired up, gettin' more angry by the minute and mad enough to spit fire. About the time that these fellas was walking this monument up the plank trying to get it up and it's taking forever, Grampa jumped off that wagon and he went over there and he knocked all them fellas right out of the way.

He said, "You can't do nothin' right anyway. Get out of the road! Let a man put that on there fer ya."

He grabbed that monument and flung it right up on the back of that wagon. And the wagon 'bout squatted, ya know.

They picked themselves up and got the plank.

And he said, "Now get out of the road so I can get to work. I've waited here long enough for you fellers."

So when I was a kid, every time I couldn't lift something, my father would always tell how strong Grampa was. And I'm grunting and groaning and trying to get this rock up out of the ground or a log on the wagon.

He would always tell me it was a good thing that my grandfather couldn't see me because ". . . he was the strongest darn man in the North Country, you know. Why his wrist was six inches wide . . ."

Well, when I grew up and got married, I'd heard all these stories about milkmen. And there came an ad in the paper for a job for a milkman. I wanted to see if any of them stories was true or not, so I took that job.

I was a milkman for about three or four years. I used to stop every other day at this old gentlemen's house, down in Hanawah. His name was Llewellen Snyder. He used to run a speakeasy there in Hanawah and they brought booze across the border from Canada over to the speakeasy, made bathtub gin and a little home brew and that sort of

5

stuff. He had an old house. It had twelve-inch walls. They had big casings and the window sills were big enough to put lots of plants and stuff in. He'd clear that window sill out and sit in his rocking chair with his shawl blanket sort of around him. He was real old, ninety-five and more probably.

He had in that window sill—no plants—but he had all these dice and all these cards and pictures of ladies of the night that used to come up to entertain the loggers on the weekends. They came from Utica, these women did. They'd come up by train and stage and whatever, get up there entertain the loggers on the weekends and take the loggers money and then they'd go back for a few days and then some more would come on the next weekend. That was the rotation of the thing.

Of course these dice were all crooked. Some only rolled sevens and some rolled snake eyes and some rolled elevens and he knew every one of them dice by name, almost by heart, and what it was going to roll whenever you threw it.

He had all these cards and he'd say, "Now that's the ace of spades or that's this or that's that." And he'd say, "See that little dot?" Or there'd be a little curvature in the decoration on the outside of that card. Just the difference of one little line. He knew every one of them by heart and all them cards. Whenever you sat there with a handful of cards in front of this man, he knew exactly what you were holding.

All this stuff was in there, and he'd go through all that memorabilia every time I would stop with the milk. He'd show me something new every time. Oh, he was wonderful. It went on two years, two and a half years.

I stopped there one day and he said, "You know I've been thinkin' about you."

I said "You have?"

He said "Yes, you're Billy Smith."

I said, "Yes!"

6

"Why you're Roy Smith's boy, aren't ya? And you must be one of the young ones."

I said, "Yeah, I'm the youngest one."

He said, "Then you're from the Featherbed."

I said, "Yes."

He said, "You're Peter Smith's grandson."

I said "Yes".

"Strongest man in this North Country", he said. "Did you know that his wrist was six inches wide?"

I said, "Yes, I certainly did know that because my father told me every twenty minutes."

"Did you ever hear about the time them Eyetalians down here had lost the monument through the wagon?" he said. "Peter jumped off there and knocked them right out of the road and throwed that monument right up on the back of that wagon. Wonder it didn't bust it all to hell," he said.

At that point I realized that my father hadn't been lying to me, that he wasn't just trying to get me to lift something, that it was a fact that my grandfather had a wrist that was six inches wide, and he was known as the strongest man in the North Country.

My father would say, "You know your grandfather was the strongest man in this North Country." The same words came out of that man's mouth, exactly as my father had said it!

THE DAPPLE GREY HORSE

Now Grandpa Smith was a horse trader. He did a lot of horse swapping and dickering. He was a man who knew all the tricks and passed them on to his sons, of course. My father was known around as a pretty good horseman and horse trader who knew a good horse when he saw one. He was the guy that could pick out a decent horse. If somebody wasn't too good and was a greenhorn at this, they might go to my father and say, "Go with me and pick out a horse," because he was a guy you could rely on to pick you out a good horse. Well, he was very superstitious. A lot of superstitions and ghost stories and witch stories and all these things arose from the Scottish ancestry. He wouldn't keep a white horse very long because it could be hazardous to your health. A white horse was something that might have been related back to the old witch stories of the devil horse, maybe, and a white horse might have been a descendent of these horses that the devil had. If you took a load of hay in on a fork some night to feed this horse he might bite you in the jugular and you'd bleed to death before you ever got out of there. Or he might kick you in the head and knock your brains out and kill you. Or he might just plain squish you up against the stall until you just died. So a white horse wasn't anything that anybody with superstition would want to keep around very long.

My father had taken in this really nice white horse in a trade, but he didn't want to keep it. He had a dapple gray horse that he just thought the world of.

Everywhere he went he'd say, "I've got a white horse over there. If anybody wants to trade for a dapple horse just like this one to mate, I'm trying

to mate them up. And I'll swap them that white horse: he's a good un. He'd make you a good horse, a good solid horse."

It wasn't long, a couple weeks, when my father got a letter in the mail. It was a feller down in Norwood who dealt in horses. The letter said,

> *Roy,*
>   *I understand you're looking for a dapple horse. I've seen that white horse and he is a good horse. I wouldn't mind swappin' ya. We've got a dapple horse down here that's the spittin' image of yours. If you want to bring that white horse down on the weekend, why maybe we can make a deal.*

My mother said that when the weekend rolled around, he was getting real fidgety. He got up real early, did his chores, and she knew right away he wanted to go down and swap them horses.

She made up a picnic lunch and right after chores he said, "What do you say we go down there and see if we can make a deal on that horse?"

My mother loaded everything in the buggy and my father got the white horse hooked up right off quick. They piled right in the buggy and down they went. It took the better part of the forenoon. They stopped and had a little lunch just before they got there outside of town and went on in to take a look at the horse.

My father pulled the old white horse up to the old hitching post, went in and he found the guy in charge. He started down through there and they finally got down to where this dapple horse was. My father fell in love with that horse the minute he looked at it.

These fellows, they all have a ritual that they go through. Whether they know what they're doing or not, they always have to go through this. They've got to prove to the other guy that they know what they're doing, see. The first thing that they do is examine that horse, sort of physical examination

10

type thing. Grab the horse by the nose put a thumb in one side and a finger in the other side and kind of pull up in the nose and grab the horse by that hangy down thing on the chin there and yank down until the horse's mouth would open up. Then they would check those teeth. Now they had to be just the right length. My father claimed he could tell the age of a horse within twenty minutes just by the length of those teeth. And so he checked all them teeth out and then of course they seemed to be just fine and he run his fingers up the horse's nose. That was the next thing, look around in there to see if there was any lumps or bumps or abscesses or anything. That horse was sneezing and taking on and pounding his feet and throwing his tail and throwing his head and every-thing because it was driving him crazy with that finger stuck up his nose.

Poor horse, by this time his eyes were already watering up and now it was time to check his eyes to see if he could see or not. They'd take a wooden match out of their pocket, and wind that horse's eyelid up on that match, and roll it right up there, and then he could look around in the horse's cheeks and move things around and make the horse roll his eyes. Then they'd pull that match out and that eyelid would plop back down there. Water would be running down the horse's eyes and then he'd stand back and make motions at the poor thing's eyes. If he blinked, well they knew he could see something. And so he was in pretty good shape with the eyesight and all that. They checked the ears out and run their fingers down in the horse's ears and about in there—see?—for anything that might be wrong down in there. And then they'd run around back of the horse and clap their hands and make a loud noise, stamp their feet or something. If the horse flinched, well they knew he could hear. And then they'd go down his neck and down his shoulders and down his legs and feel for any bruis-es, bone splints or anything—or maybe he'd been

11

punched in the foot with a stub sometime or other in the woods. Check all that, pick the horse's foot up. I remember when I was a little kid, all of them had a jack knife, a pen knife, and they'd run that around the horse's frog in his foot and clean the manure out. They'd flick that manure in a kid's face if he got too close, to keep him away cause they didn't want him around where they was, in case the horse would start jumping or kicking or something. He checked the frog out on the horse's foot and all that, checked the shoes and the nails and everything to make sure they were all right and the horse didn't have sore feet. Everything was fine.

Then he went down to the side of the horse. Now this was important because some of them old timers would take a real skinny horse that was in bad shape and they'd blow him up. And so they wanted to make sure that that was real fat on the horse and not air. They would take a little air pump, something like what you'd blow up a football up with, put a hypodermic needle in the end of it and they would stick it in the horse's hide. They would start blowing in different spots and move it about until the horse looked like he was rolled in fat. There was nothing but air under there. When you struck that with your fist the air would move about and you knew it wasn't real, so he hit the horse on the side and almost knocked the poor thing sideways and nothing moved. If it was good solid meat and not air, he knew the horse was in good shape. Go down the back legs—same as the front legs—and check all that out. Check the hind feet and everything same as he did the front. And then go around behind the horse and start rolling their sleeve up and pulling up the horse's tail and checking for worms and that sort of thing. This is all something you did from the side 'cause the horse could kick you. He checked all that business. That horse was as sound as a million dollars.

Next thing was to check him for heaves, took

12

him out of the barn, exchanged him for the white horse. They took the white horse off wherever they took white horses off to. He hooked that gray horse on to the buggy there. Heaves is a lung disorder. If they got it very bad, if you run them for about fifteen minutes, it'll show up. And so he put him on there and run him around the block there about fifteen minutes or so, probably a half a dozen times or so. When they got back that horse was probably breathing better than my father was. He was in great shape. There wasn't anything wrong with that horse at all.

My father said, "Emily, give me the money for the difference between them horses." Now my mother was the boss of the family. She carried all the money and everything. My father didn't want the responsibility. She gave him the money. He walked about fifty foot over there and give it to the guy for the horse as if he had it in his pocket all the while. He went over there and paid him for the horse.

When he got back in the buggy, he said to my mother, he said "Boy, Emily, I beat the pants off that guy this time! I really got him good this time. This is a real good horse, lot better than that white horse."

And so they headed for home. They got up around Hanawah and up along the Racquet River. You could see it was getting late, anyway, but it was exceptionally dark up there and it was starting to lightening. And as they got up the Racquet River further they run into this heavy, heavy thunder and lightening storm. It was coming right down pitchforks, hammer and tongs. It was just really in torrents.

My mother said you could drive right along behind that horse and watch it change colors right before your eyes. When they got home they had the most beautiful white horse you ever saw in your life. I guess the guy had dyed that horse and put them dapples on there.

13

The old timers would take ashes and soot and a hard boiled egg and they'd wet the hard boiled egg and roll it in a different mixture of ashes and soot and they could roll them gray dots right on to the back of that horse you see, paint them right up in good shape and they'd last 'till it rained, or 'till they rolled in the dirt and that was the end of it, of course. They could make a white horse into a dapple horse real easy.

THE NEW HARNESS

Now my father had many horses through his lifetime, but one time he got this really nice buggy horse. Even though my father had a Model T Ford car, my folks still liked to hook up a horse and go for a ride into the village. Besides, where we lived, most folks still had horses and buggies.

My father bought a nice new buggy and a nice trotting harness [or buggy harness] with brass fittings and the whole works to go with this great horse he had. Well, one day the folks took the old car and went to Potsdam to do some shopping and they left the kids at home. The oldest ones were to watch the rest.

Ma and Pa spent the day in Potsdam. They had to get home in time to get the milking and other chores under way. Well, our old house was near a very sharp corner of the road. Now, when the folks came to that corner they saw pieces of broken buggy parts in the road and along the stone wall by the road side, and there were pieces of leather harness along the way as well.

"Somebody must have been going pretty fast around that bend and didn't make it," Pa said. "I hope their horse is all right."

Well, when they got home, the kids didn't come running down to the car to help bring in the goods or see if they had got some candy or something for being good, so my mother called up to the house, "Come down here and help out!" Kids started limping out of the house and heading down to the car.

Well, the folks weren't long looking for my father's good buggy and it was gone. It seems that the older kids hooked the big bull up to that buggy with my father's brand new buggy harness and all the other kids got on board, off they went flying across the meadow right through the field of oats and when that bull come to the stone wall, he jumped it, right out into the road, leaving pieces of buggy and harness all over that stone wall and the road.

Kids were scattered clean down to Will Newton's driveway.

So much for the new harness.

HABIT'S A GREAT THING

We never went hungry in our lives. We were always well fed. We lived right off the land, but we knew what we were doing. Now we used to, of course, get all this venison stuff and all that. Well my father learned about this during the depression. World War II was going on when I was a little kid and times were really hard. Maybe you liked to hunt. Maybe you had to eat a lot of venison and stuff, but you didn't have any way of way of buying shells to shoot them with because you couldn't buy a bullet or shell anywhere, or cartridge—as the old timers call them, *cahtridges*. They had to figure out a way to get that venison without shooting cartridges.

My father, he wasn't anybody's fool. He had a rail fence that run between the cow pasture and the back yard. Anybody that lived out in the country and went barefoot as much as we did would have a rail fence between the cow pasture and the backyard with all them meadow muffins around and stuff. You might be running out to the privy at three o'clock in the morning and barefoot, step right in the middle of one of them things and not hit the ground much 'fore daylight, so you didn't want them in your back yard.

He had this rail fence there. Why not take advantage of a good rail fence? He'd get salt and he'd salt them top rails on that fence. Five or six deer around there, they'd get the habit of running right down and licking on them rails along in the summer. Well, by fall there were ten to fifteen down there every night licking on them rails. Along just before Christmas or so, there'd be twenty-five or thirty of them coming down there every night licking on them rails.

My father had it all figured out. He did every-thing by the moon. He planted all his crops by the moon. Everything that grew under the ground was planted by the black of the moon. Everything that grew on top of the ground was planted in the full of the moon or the white of the moon. We always fig-ured that's why us kids was all born in the same month, because he did everything by the moon. We made a good go of it though, and he'd watch that moon and just before Christmas along after Thanksgiving, he'd start watching. He knew when the moon got high that it was going to drop down to thirty below zero or so. We had this big Coca Cola thermometer that was on the side of the barn out there. He'd watch that thermometer. It was only registered for twenty-five below. He had trou-ble with it because every time it dropped down to thirty-five or forty below it would pull that darn thermometer right off the side of the barn! And so one day he got discouraged and he nailed it up there with railroad spikes, drove it right in to the timbers in the barn there on the inside. He said, "That ought to hold it."

It dropped down to forty below that night and pretty near killed two of his best work horses. Pulled that corner of the barn right down into the ground there. And the horses were in that corner and it like to squished the two horses. I don't know if you ever tried to feed a horse through a knot hole or not: it's not an easy trick. It run on about three or four days before we could get that corner of the barn jacked up and get them horses out of there.

Anyway, he'd watch that moon. When it got up big and high, why he'd say, "Well boys, I think tonight's the night we're going to get our *venson*. It's going to drop down about forty below tonight, a good night to get some venson."

Us boys knew what to do. We'd go out and take them salty rails off the top of that fence, take them in the barn and lean them up in the corner. Then we'd go in to the other side of the barn where Pa kept them big sixteen-foot long, four-inch iron pipes. About eight of us would haul them iron pipes out there and fling them in where them rails was. Habit's a great thing, you know, and if you take advantage of it you can catch animals with habit. Them deer would come running down there that night, forty below zero. We'd all be in there sleeping. We'd get up in the morning and go out there, and there'd be about ten or fifteen deer all stuck by their tongues onto those iron pipes. My mother would come running out there with a tea kettle of warm water in one hand and a ball bat in the other. If they had horns sticking out of them, why she'd take the ball bat to them and make them into meat. If they were does and fawns, why she would just pour some warm water on their tongues and they'd go bouncing back off into the woods there. Those does were good lookers, because it wouldn't only be about two or three nights and they'd be back with more bucks.

That's how we used to keep in *venson* when you couldn't buy any *cahtridges*.

NEW GAME WARDEN

Now we'd lived up there on that Featherbed all the while and pretty much had our own way about things. We'd been always eating, as we call it, a lot of *venson*. We don't have an *i* in *venson* the way we pronounce it. We ate lots of it. We ate it the year round. We used to go out and shoot deer whenever we felt like we needed to. We would cut the meat up and pack it into quart jars so tight that you couldn't get any more in. You'd take one piece of stuff that wasn't very good and you'd put it right on the top and put a teaspoon of salt on it per quart. Screw the lid down real tight and fill your pack basket full of that stuff and take it out and bury it in the muck in the bottom of the springs in the mountains where the game wardens couldn't find it. (Neighbors or somebody would steal it if they found it too, you know.) If you wanted to keep it and not get in trouble, that's where you kept it. You'd bury it in the muck and it would last for years. It was as fresh as the day you put it in there. It'd be just as red and nice, just as fresh. Raw meat. The idea was packing it tight so no air was in it and putting the salt in the top and screwing the lid down tight. And it was submerged under the water in the muck in the bubbling springs. It just lasted forever. It just was so good. It tasted so fresh. It was just like you went out and shot it, a year later. The piece on top was a piece of flank . . . something that wasn't a great cut, something you'd have ground into hamburger, probably . . . You just lay that on top, put a teaspoon of salt on it. That's the first thing out—throw that to the cat. Then the rest of it's all good going.

Whenever my mother would want a jar or two or three or five or six jars of venson, she'd say to us kids, "Take the pack basket and go over to one of them springs there and get a jar of venson. Don't go to the same spring you went to last time. Don't leave a trail, now. Don't want anyone finding it." We were taught at a young age how to go in to the woods without leaving a lot of tracks. We'd get the venson and bring it back and she'd have a big old venson feed. We were used to that way of life. We got a brand new game warden. Now the old game wardens knew we had a big family and they were used to turning their head. They didn't ask a lot of questions, but we didn't know about this new game warden. He wasn't around here probably a month and we knew what his tire tracks looked like and what his shoe tracks looked like, and what the sound of his car sounded like coming down the cobblestone road, and approximately how fast he drove and what he looked like and what he wore most of the time. We knew a lot about this man. The poor man, of course, he probably didn't have any idea he was being watched anywhere near as close as he was. But we wanted to know about this fellow.

My mother had planned this great summer get-together, a family reunion. All the brothers and sisters, aunts and uncles and nephews and nieces and cousins, and all them folks would be coming to this great get together. Well, we had some neighbors that were known to steal things. And they wasn't ashamed about getting in your chicken coop. My mother had these roosters and a couple of ducks or geese that she had planned on having for this get together. And just about a week before the reunion, the birds all come up missing. Somebody had stolen them. We had to have something for this dinner and we didn't have any money to buy anything with. My brother worked in logging, drawing logs in and out of the woods all the time with the log truck.

"I'll get you something for your reunion, Ma," he

said, "I'll get you a couple deer and you can have the venson."

He come back in a couple days and pulled up in by the barn with a load of pulpwood. "Come help me unload this pulpwood out here," he said. We got in the middle of the truck and dug down about half way in that middle tier and there was two deer laying there. We took them in the barn and cut them up.

The weekend rolled around and Ma's having this big venson feed. Everybody came and pulled off to the side of the driveway and parked in the meadow. She figured that everybody was there that was going to be there. It was in the late summertime—late August or early September and it was hot in that kitchen. The cook stove was going and she'd been baking bread and pies and all that stuff. There was venson on that stove going, some with onions and some with mushrooms and some with whatever way you wanted to fix it. There was venson stew going and all kinds of stuff going on the back of that stove—all that venson and of course illegal as all get out.

My father was a nervous little guy. He was always saying, "This is the time you're going to get caught." And he was the first one to say, "Well, we're out of meat. Somebody ought to go get a deer, you know. We've got to get some more meat here, pretty quick."

Well, somebody'd go get a deer. Then, when they'd got it, he'd say, "By golly, you want to be careful. This is the time you're going to get caught, you know." He would go on with this thing every time. He had done that this time too, so he was real nervous about the whole thing. We're all standing around there laughing and joking. The girls were setting the table and the boys are lugging in more wood for the stove. Everything is going on normal like.

All at once we heard this car pull in the driveway. And my father said, "Geez, I thought every-body was here. Wonder who that is?"

Pa went out on the porch to see who it was. He let out a holler out and come running back in the house. "Emily, that new game warden is coming right up the driveway!"

He flew back into that house. He grabbed the griddles off that stove and he flung that venson right into that stove. The fire went up into the air and it caught all the grease on fire. Meat was burning and the little ashes were coming back down and fire was going all over the place. He grabbed them frying pans, flung them into that open oven door, slammed the oven door shut with his foot, whirled and went out that door to meet the game warden before he got up into the porch. The game warden just backed out of the driveway and drove back toward Colton. He was turning around—or else he smelled the meat and he wasn't going to bother us.

What happened, I have no idea, but he left and my father had completely ruined Sunday dinner. He come running back in and said, "He's gone! He's gone! Get them long-handled forks."

My mother said, "We already got forks." You could smell hair burning and singeing, everybody reaching in at the same time trying to get that meat out of there. My mother salvaged the bucket of stew that was on the back of the stove and headed for the woodshed with that. That was salvaged, but the rest of it was all pretty well scorched.

For some reason we weren't supposed to have that family reunion that day.

REVEREND WATERSON'S WOOD PILE

Reverend Waterson was a friend of my father's. He was quite a neat guy. By "neat," I mean clean and well groomed. His pants always had such a crease in them that you could almost cut your finger on it. His shoes were always as shiny as patent leather, but they were polished—they weren't patent leather shoes. He'd stop by and give a little prayer once in a while, but they were just plain friends anyway.

My father used to sell a lot of wood. We always had wood piled out back seasoning away. He got a letter from Rev. Waterson saying, "If you're down this way, Roy, drop off a cord of wood for me."

Rev. Waterson was really a perfectionist. Everything was in its place throughout his place. The yard was always spic and span. The house was just so clean you could eat right off the floor.

My father thought, "Well, I'm not going to go there for a cord of wood, but when the time comes I get another order or something, I'll go down and I'll drop it off." It went on a while, and he got a letter from a couple old ladies that had retired from teaching school. They lived down in Colton, over the other side of the river. They wanted to know if Roy would bring them down a couple cord of wood, sometime when he was coming down.

So he thought, "For three cord of wood, I'll load it on the sled and take it down." The weekend rolled around and he loaded the wood on the sled and took it on down there and pulled up into the old ladies' driveway. He went over there first. He figured he'd stop and visit with Rev. Waterson on the way back a little bit. He didn't want to kill time on the way over. He went right over there first, pulled right up into the driveway. There was a clothesline across there with some clothes on it, scared the horses. They didn't want to go by it (or) under it. My father had to stop the horses there, and that meant he was going to have to carry that wood a little further than what he wanted to.

All these old houses had the woodshed that came off the back, one with a little trap door like a little slide door or a little door that flopped up and down, or had a little knob on it or some little thing. That door would open—it would stay open somehow or other so you could throw the wood through it. He was about, probably fifty foot away from that door, not too far. Far enough that he carried the wood and threw it through. It was only a couple cord. He started hauling the wood over, and threw it through the hole. The minute the wood hit the woodshed floor them women heard that and out they come. Had on their boots and their coats. They'd heard stories about those wood dealers and they weren't going to take any chances on this guy beatin' them or anything. They were watching him every move he made. They came outdoors and they followed him from the sled to the woodshed, back to the sled, back to the woodshed, back to the sled, back to the woodshed.

"Roy, is this beech—this gray one?"

"Yup, that's beech."

"That's good wood, isn't it, Roy?"

"Yes, that burns real good."

"Well, this white one, that shouldn't be in there, Roy. That's birch, I know what that is. That don't burn too well."

"That burns just fine," my father said, "as long as it's mixed with the other hardwoods and stuff. And you gotta have something in there to keep the fire going so that the other wood will catch. And it's important that its mixed in there with that."

He tried to explain all that stuff to them. Well, they didn't want to listen. They thought sure that they were getting beat on this and beat on that. He was getting pretty well fed up with all that business. He had sort of a short fuse, so he thought, "Well I'll go inside and pile some of it and maybe

25

they'll leave me alone." So he went in and he started piling up the wood.

They come right in and they started asking him more questions. "You sure that's high enough? You sure that's eight foot long? You sure that that's the way you're supposed to do this?"

He was still being driven crazy.

Finally one of them said, "Roy, by the way, how much is that wood going to cost anyway?"

My father says, "Well, I've been charging a dollar and a half a cord."

One of the women said, "Emma, did you hear that? A dollar and a half a cord! Wouldn't that just take your breath?"

Well, when she said that my father flung that wood down there.

He said, "Lady, if you had to go out to cut that wood with a cross cut saw; split it; pile it up out there; wait for it to season; throw it in the sleds; bring it down here; throw it through that cheesly hole over there; then throw it in here and come in here and pile it up," he said, "Yes, it would take your breath, no question about it!" He was pretty upset.

Well, they finally paid him and he went on his way. He got over to Rev. Waterson's, the perfectionist, and there was two posts driven in the ground exactly eight foot long and exactly four foot high. He pulled up to them posts. When he started to take the remainder of that wood off the sleds and fill it in between them posts, he realized them women had talked him right out of more wood than he wanted to give them. He had given them more than two cord and he didn't have a full cord to give Rev. Waterson. So he piled it real loose: I call it "the Adirondack way of pilin' wood."

When he got through he had all this wood in there that filled the full space, eight foot long and four foot high, but you could throw the cat right through that wood pile anywhere. It was full of air holes. He went around back and Mrs. Waterson paid him and he went home.

26

It run on about a week, and he got a letter from Rev. Waterson:

Dear Roy,
   You know the Good Lord furnishes air for nothing. I don't see why I gotta pay a dollar and a half a cord for it.

SCOTTISH BILL MCCLAIN

Now when a young fella would go to work in the loggin' camps, these old timers knew you quit school and went to work in the woods. They'd try to get you to go back to school, get you to get an education so you would become something and wouldn't have to kill yourself working yourself to death. They weren't above givin' you a crack side the head if they thought that would get you mad enough to quit and go back to school. All these young guys were determined. They were stubborn and they weren't going to do anything but what they wanted to do. And at that particular time they wanted to work in the woods. So they'd fight back.

This is a poem that I made up from some of my father's experiences and some of my own. I thought there needed to be a eulogy to the men that's been killed in the logging camps.

I went to work in a loggin' camp when I was seven-
teen
Up in back of Saranac for Jones and Hammerstein.
Walked into the bunk house, as cocky as could be,
And threw my duffel right down on the first bunk
that I see.

Them loggers started laughin' and givin' me the eye.
And that's when someone struck me, sort of took me
by surprise.
I went down on my backside like I'd been struck by
a train.
And I looked up about seven foot and saw Scottish
Bill McClain.

He said, "What the hell is a greenhorn doing on me
bunk?
You want it, lad, you'll have to fight for it—if you
think you've got the spunk."

Then he grabbed me by the hair and yanked me
    across the floor,
He said, "Well laddie, have you had enough or
    would you like some more?"

Well, I reached my hand out to him as though I were
    nearly dead,
And when he reached down to pull me up. I kicked
    him in the head.
He went about ten steps backwards and was bleed-
    in' from the nose,
And hit his head there on that bunk and wilted like
    a rose.

Well, we got a dipper of water and threw it in his
    face.
And he looked me right square in the eye,
And he said, "Well, laddie you win that race.
Ain't too often you see a greenhorn that's got that
    kind of spunk,
So I guess it's only proper that you get the gol-
    darned bunk."

I said, "No, that's your bunk." And I went to the
    other side,
And I gathered out my duffel and I left him with his
    pride.
Later on that night we shook hands and I told him
    my name.
He said, "I'm proud to meet ya, lad. Mine's Scottish
    Bill McClain."

We worked together about nine years. We were
    friendly just like kids.
He taught me how to chop and saw and how to roll
    and skid.
He taught me how to peel pulp and brush the skid-
    way out.
Wherever you'd see one of us, you'd find the other,
    no doubt.

One day we were fallin' pine about three foot on a
    stump,
When the wind blew wrong and I saw old Bill drop
    the saw and jump.

I looked up just to see that big tree turning back.
I tried to run but my foot was caught,, and couldn't
   get no slack.

Well, old Bill saw what was happening, he turned
   and ran at me,
He said, "I'll get ya, laddie!" And then he pushed
   me free,
But old Bill lost his footin'. He slipped and then fell
   down
Just as that big pine tree come crashing to the
   ground.

Well, in a moment it was over and the dust had
   cleared away,
And I knew that Scottish Bill McClain had met his
   judgment day.
For that big pine tree had fallen on him and had
   pinned him to the ground,
So I called for some of the other boys to come and
   help around.

We sawed and chopped and got him out and took
   him to the camp
And built a coffin for him by the light of a kerosene
   lamp.
Next day we had a readin', and we laid old Bill to
   rest
In his brand new sidewalk clothes, his watch and
   chain and vest.

We took his boots and his old brown hat and hung
   them on a cross.
That was placed at the foot of old Bill's grave and
   driven in the moss.
And there upon a pine tree we carved in, good and
   plain,
"He gave his life to help his friend, old Scottish Bill
   McClain."

NOTES

This is the man's world—not of Bill's generation—but of Bill's father's, who was born in the 1880's. Bill's parents were almost old enough to be his grandparents. With the older children out on their own, Roy and Emily Smith had more time, and the incentive of a changing outside world, to make sure their youngest learned the old ways. Through tall tales and good talk, the format and motifs of the old yarns were passed on, along with with traditional ruses and practical jokes, as a valued part of everyday life. For structural analysis of the traditional folktale see Stith Thompson, The Folktale. *[1946. Reprint Berkeley: University of California Press, 1977].* Richard Bauman, Verbal Art as Performance. *[Prospect Height, Ill.: Waveland Press, 1977] looks at functions and context.*

Local legends spring up around the strong, the clever, the proud and the stupid. Sometimes they are true, like the story of Peter Smith and the gravestones. Sometimes travelling Paul Bunyan-like motifs are worked into the true story. In tellings as good as Bill's, you can't see the seam where the old story is patched into the new cloth.

Sometimes, travelling trickster jokes are actually re-enacted. They are always told for true. The story of the painted horse is enjoyed among horse traders world-wide. Who can tell when—or if—it actually happened? The importance of the story isn't about literal fact, anyway. Stories like "The Dapple-Grey Horse," are one sort of cautionary tale, warning the apprentice trader about dangers of gullibility and pride. Jan Harold Brunvand's The Vanishing Hitchhiker: American Urban Legends and Their Meanings. *[New York and London: W.W. Norton and Co.,1981] observes that the stories ". . . reflect simple human misjudgment, bad luck, and an artistic exploration in oral tradition of the possibilities of things."*

Sometimes real life well-remembered is the tallest tale of all. The elder Smith children did wreck the buggy. Roy Smith really planted by the moon. Did the Smith family really add to their winter meat supply as advertised? Beats me!

The tall tale device Gilbert Ryle calls the category mistake is as old as Herodotus and Aristophanes. A category mistake ". . . creates an absurdity by allocating an object or concept to a logical type or category to which it does not belong," for example, the assigning of human thinking to animals. Did the does bring back more bucks? If they did, they're kin to the snow snakes that bring ice fishermen bait in exchange for whiskey! See Carolyn S. Brown, The Tall Tale in American Folklore and Literature. [Knoxville: University of Tennessee Press, 1987.]

"The New Game Warden," and "Rev. Waterson's Woodpile" set up the hill folks' relations to three different sets of outsiders. Rev. Waterson's letter is a traditional retort told for true. Is it true? What's truth?

Celtic people have a centuries-old recitation tradition. The Smith family's Scots stories and beliefs [the white horse as bad luck, for example] are Scottish by way of Canada. Margaret Bennett's warm and thorough study, The Last Stronghold: Scottish Gaelic Traditions in Newfoundland. [St. John's, Newfoundland: Breakwater Books, 1989.] shows us how these traditions operate in daily life.

Bill remembers recitations from his family and neighbors. In the mid-1980's, Bill spent a year recording more stories and recitations from older Adirondack masters under a grant funded by the Folk Arts Program of the New York State Council on the Arts. Bill brought Harvey Carr [I Was on the Wrong Bear. Greenfield Review Press, 1992] to my attention. Bill recognized the importance of his neighbor, master raconteur Ham Ferry who held court behind the bar of Ham's Inn down the road at

Childwold. Bill spent a winter listening to Ham, learning how to tell recitations in the old way.

"Scottish Bill McClain," Bill's own work, is in the Celtic woods tradition. If you hear echoes of Robert Service ["Spell of the Yukon," "The Cremation of Sam McGee"] in Bill's cadences, you're hearing correctly. Bill, and many other North Country woodsmen, know Service recitations by heart. Often they learned them, not from books, but from other woodsmen. There are two reissues of Service poems: The Best of Robert Service *[Philadelphia: Running Press, 1990], and* The Collected Poems of Robert Service *[New York: Putnam Publishing Group, 1989].*

As he gets older, Bill says he wakes up in the night making up new poems!

SHE HAD A BIG LOOK

*The major purpose of the comedian is
to remind us how deeply rooted we are in
all the tangible things of this world.*

—Nathan A. Scott—

*Character has always been
the great American subject.*

—Constance Rourke—

DO IT YOURSELF PRACTICE

When I was a kid, my mother and I went to Potsdam one day. You went across this bridge, and then you crossed another bridge. That was The Island in there. There was a big church on it. The Montgomery Ward's store was right across the river.

There was an iron picket fence that went around that Montgomery Ward's store right by the river. The steam came up out of there and there was always a lot of frost on them iron pickets. We got right across the bridge there one day and there was all these kids from French Village screaming and hollering and yelling. Oh! It was an awful noise!

And my mother said, "Something's wrong with one of them kids." So we went running right over there and one kid had his tongue stuck on one of them iron spikes that stuck up there. He had ripped that tongue just about half off. It was bleeding something awful. My mother tried to calm him down, got him calmed down some, and got the other kids out of the way and done screaming and hollering.

She said, "I'll take care of it. You just get back out of the way now." She cupped her hands and blew over the kid's tongue, and kept blowing in there, and took spit and put it on there. She had these squirrel-lined gloves that somebody had bought her for driving gloves. She took those and she cupped them around. She blew in there and she finally thawed that kid's tongue out, got him unhooked. He was bleeding pretty bad.

She said, "You go tell your mother and get to a doctor right soon as you can."

They all went running across that bridge. Never

saw them again. I always wondered what happened to that kid, whether his tongue fell off or they got it sewed back on. I was seven or eight. It was that age where I would be sticking my tongue on something. It really scared me.

My mother was used to kids. She gave some of the first mouth-to-mouth resuscitation that ever was given in these parts. About sixty years ago, when Richard was a little baby, my mother had started a fire with a kerosene can. You take an old tomato can and you squeeze it so it made a pouring spout. Put kerosene in it and use it to start the fire with. She set it on the oven door.

Well, she was busy. Time went by and the stove got real hot. The kitchen got hot. And that can set there. It was making a vapor coming from it now, because it was real warm. Richard pulled himself up there by the oven door. He smelled of that vapor and he went out like a light. On his back he went and turned perfectly blue and everything. Couldn't breathe, couldn't breathe at all. He just was dead. He laid there as limp as a rag and as blue as anything. Something just told my mother that if she could blow into his mouth and into his nose that she could get some good air into his lungs, that she had to get some good air into his lungs and drive that stuff out of there. She just started blowing into his mouth. She said you could see him bloat right up as she was blowing right into him. She said she quit and the air would come out and she'd blow some more. And she'd quit and the air would come out and she'd blow some more. She was doing everything except compressions and she didn't have any idea that that was what you did to save somebody's life.

He came around after a while. Took him down to Doc Swart's. Doc Swart said, "Well, you saved his life. That's all there is to it. That's an amazing thing, but if you hadn't done that he never would have lived." And, of course, Doc Swart learned something, too.

It's survival. It's do it yourself practice. She was used to doing everything herself. She wasn't used to running to someone else for answers. If she had to come up with one, then she would come up with it. That was just the case of her coming up with another answer to something. Everybody will tell you that's what she did.

SHE AIN'T AFRAID OF NOTHIN'

Ira Irish was a little guy that did odd chores all the while. He'd come and split your wood for you or he'd lug your water for you or he'd help paint your house or things. Everybody considered Ira as not having both oars in the water, but Ira turned out to know more than folks thought he did.

Ira predicted a lot of things. He didn't really predict it, he said he *did* it. He had his own little space-ship; he used to go to the moon every little while. It very much resembled the Challenger and these things they are going to the moon with today. He would explain all this stuff to you and he'd sit there. He had eyelashes that were sort of white, and blue eyes. He looked as if he was—well—inner bred, you know. I don't think he was. He just was a neat little guy.

Ira could tell you the darndest stories. One time, I remember sitting when I was a kid listening to him at the kitchen table. He was telling my father how he hadn't been to the house for two or three months or something. Been gone somewheres—not far, though, you know, 'cause he never left this neck of the woods. He couldn't read or write, so you knew he didn't get this out of books.

Well, he sat there one day at the kitchen table, and my father says, "Where ya been?"

He said, "Well, I've been working up in Maine," he said.

"Oh," my father said, "Working in a lumber camp?"

"Yup, working in a loggin' camp—up in Maine." And he said, "Boy," he said, "you ought to see the machines they got up there. You don't have to skid logs with horses up there."

"They've got machines that do it up there?"

"They got a big machine up there," he said. "It's so big it has to bend in the middle in order to get around the trees," he said, "can't even get it around the trees. The tires are so big on it, they stand so high it takes two men setting on the top of each other's shoulders to reach the top of the tires." And he says, "Got a big machine on the back with a big chain on there that you can snake up three or four whole trees at a time. Drag the whole tree right up to the skidway."

My father was laughing. He thought that was just hilarious. Today you got a machine that bends in the middle because it can't get around the trees otherwise. The tires are so high that two men can't reach the top. It's got a huge thing in the back that can pull up four or five trees at a clip. And it's called a *skidder*. Ira identified a skidder right to the tee. Where did he get that from? All the things that everybody laughed at Ira for when I was a kid are true today. Unbelievable.

Ira was at the house one time, and he was splitting wood—a big wood pile just flung in a heap down there by the barn. Ira would split that wood in his own time. He would come take his breaks and my mother would give him switchell and stuff and keep him from hurting himself, splitting too much wood. She took good care of him 'cause he was a nice little guy. He was out there splittin' wood, had his bib overalls on and had his blue work shirt buttoned up tight around his neck, of course. That was the dress of the times. He would wear his work shoes or a pair of rubber boots up to his knees.

Had his ax. Everybody split wood with an ax. They didn't use one of them wood-splitting mauls like they do today, they just had a regular ax. If you twist your ax just when you hit the block of wood, that wood will pop right apart and it will fly all over the place. It's amazing to see somebody split wood and do it right. It was just part of an everyday rou-

41

tine with Ira. He could split that wood like nobody's business.

My mother was busy in the kitchen. She could look out through the front room window and see Ira. She could see part of the barn, but she couldn't see all the way up to the barn. Ira would raise his leg every time he'd go to strike that block of wood. He'd let a horrible roar out, *Hurraaaaa!* and he would bring that ax down. When he did, boy, pieces of wood would fly in all directions. He'd pick them up and he'd bend over and get them and put them in the pile. Pile them up.

Well, he got to where he'd bend over there and all at once he'd throw the ax and jump in the air and grab himself by the backside and run around in circles two or three times, pull the back of his overalls out and look down in there and reach down inside and pull his hands out—like he was pulling something out of there.

My mother thought, "What kind of shenanigans is he going through now?"

She kept an eye on him. After a while he'd bend over again to get something and oh, he'd jump in the air and grab himself by the backside and dance around in circles three or four times. My mother watched about three or four fracases of that and then she went on down there.

"What's the matter, Ira?" she said.

He said, "Bees. There's got to be a lot of bees in this wood pile. They keep stinging me on the backside."

My mother said, "Come up to the house and get a glass of switchell and take a rest. Maybe they'll be calmed down by the time you get back down. And work over on the other side of the pile a little bit. Don't disturb them. Tonight when it cools off, we'll go down and look for it and find it and throw some kerosene on it and get rid of it."

Well, Ira drank his switchell and went back out, went back down and got on the other side of the pile and started working. My mother happened to glance up and there was Ira, jumping up in the air, grabbing himself by the backside, running around in circles, same thing. The bees were still after him. She went over to look a little closer to see just what was going on. (She was starting to get really suspicious about it this time.) She noticed a movement up on the side of the barn. As she looked, she saw about four inches of a BB gun being pulled in through this knothole in the side of the barn. It was my brothers and sisters up there having fun, shooting Ira in the backside with BB's.

She went stomping down through there right by Ira and she said, "Ira, I found that bees' nest. I know right where it is. It's up in the barn."

She stomped up in the barn and up the ladder she went. And of course she flogged the heck right out of them kids and probably wrapped that BB gun right around a beam, if I know my mother. And the kids were all crying when they went out of there. You know they was. They went up around by the little brook out back and up around where Ira couldn't see them crying, on back to the house. My mother come out of there dusting off her hands and straightening up her apron and getting herself back together again after flogging the kids.

She went right up by Ira and she said "I took care of that bees' nest, Ira. You won't have to worry about no more bees bothering you."

She went on about her business and Ira went on about his business. In about three or four days my mother went in the general store over to South Colton.

The guy that was running the store, he said "Ira Irish was in here and he claims that you are one of the most powerful women in the world. He said you aren't afraid of nothing."

My mother said, "Well, I'm not afraid of anything."

He said, "Well Ira was telling how the bees was stinging him over there splitting wood, and you went right up in the hay mow, and you grabbed that bees' nest right off the peak of the barn up there in the hay mow. And you threw it right down on the barn floor and you stomped them bees all to death right there in the hay barn and killed them all off." He said, "That took quite a lot of nerve to do something like that."

My mother started laughing and she realized what it was all about. She never told Barnett the real story, you know, or anything.

She said, "Yeah," she said, "had to take care of them bees."

YOUNG BLACKSMITHS

Eddy Ciere, who was a blacksmith as well as a lumberjack and trapper, spent the weekend at our house shoeing all the horses, which my brothers and sisters watched very carefully.

One Monday morning in the summer my mother was working at the stove. The light was coming through the window on her left and she thought she saw something go by. She went and looked in time to notice that, down by the barn, one of the kids was just getting up out of the manure pile, dusting off and going into the barn through the back barn door. Well, she didn't think much of it, so she went back to work.

Before long, she saw movement go by the window again and, when she looked, another kid crawled up out of the manure pile, dusted off and went into the barn. So my mother decided to watch for a while. It wasn't long when she saw a kid fly right out of that back door of the barn, do a sort of summersault, and land sprawling in the manure pile. He got up and back in the barn he went.

Ma took off her apron, hung it on a chair and down she went.

She snuck into the barn, down in the back where Pa kept the bull. The bull was making quite a lot of fuss. When my mother got close enough, she saw four or five kids trying to put a horseshoe on that big Holstein bull. Now he was a big one. One kid would hold the bull's foot while the other kid would back up and straddle that hind leg. The other kids would hold the bull from the sides.

When the kid that was straddling that bull's leg with the horseshoe and hammer started a nail into that bull's foot . . . well things commenced to happen. That bull would straighten out with both hind

45

feet and that kid would fly right out through that door and flip right into the manure pile and they all would laugh about it. They were all having a great time: except the bull.

I wouldn't be surprised if they got in bad trouble and probably sat down real easy for a few days after that.

SHE WAS BOSS OF THE WHOLE SHEEBANG

There was a lot of colorful characters that passed through the area. My mother took care of the farm and all us kids. My mother was the boss of the whole sheebang and she was very strict and very much a lady. She wasn't a big woman, but she had a big look. You didn't mess with her, that was the impression that she would leave in your mind. She had an aura about her. She always gave us that glare when we wouldn't mind. Whenever we saw the cords in her neck, we stopped whatever we were doing, we stopped it right there. Strong, strong as a bull. She milked cows, split wood and lugged wood and carried water and worked out in the fields and grabbed a pitchfork and threw hay up on the wagon and all those things.

These drunken loggers and all kinds of people would be in and out. Loggers would come. They would go to our place because it was the pick up place for the tote wagons. The tote wagons would be running back and forth. It was so far back into the woods—it's thirty miles through the woods before you hit Cranberry Lake area. There was an upper, a middle and a lower tote road. The wagons would be gone quite a while, so these people would stay at our house for a day or two, maybe three days, waiting to catch a ride into the woods. When they came there drunk she wouldn't allow them in the house unless they knew how to behave themselves. Loggers most generally went everywhere drunk. If they had any money and access to a bar, they were going to drink. She'd make them sleep it off in the barn. They had a big table in the wood-shed where they had to put their matches and

47

their pipes and their stuff 'cause they couldn't take that stuff to the barn with them. She would let some of them in the house if they looked all right. Teddy Violet was a guy that used to come there. Teddy would come to the house on his way in and out of the woods. Now when Teddy was drunk he was an animal. He thought he was quite the ladies' man. He had about ten hands when he was drinking.

Teddy stopped there one day and he'd been drinking. My mother said, "Well sit down there, Teddy. I'll make you some black coffee and mix you up a glass of switchell and give you something to eat and get you sobered up and you can go in the other room and wait for the wagon and get straightened out."

She happened to be baking bread at the time. The big old cook stove was going. Teddy sat there drinking his switchell and his coffee and eating something. When she bent over to take the bread out, that was more than Teddy could take, having a woman bent over right there in front of him like that. So he had to reach out and pinch her on the butt.

When she come out of that oven, which she'd almost went in headlong-to, she come out of there madder than a wet hen. She went over there, and she snatched him out of that chair and straightened him up.

She said, "Mister, you're leavin'." The door opened into the corner and Teddy was blabbering about something there in his drunken stupor. And behind that door was a whole bunch of guns. And she grabbed a gun out of there and racked a shell into the barrel and stuck it right in Teddy's belly. She said, "Mister you're going and there's no question about it."

He says, "You wouldn't shoot me, would ya, Emily?"

She said, "Yes, Teddy, I'd shoot you deader than a stone. You get your satchel and your stuff, and you're leaving. You come here anytime you want when you're sober, but don't ever come to my house when you've been drinking again."

She marched him out the backyard and down to the driveway and out the driveway and started him up the road. He was mumbling and grumbling in his Irish brogue and that was the last she saw him. When he was sober, he would stop by with the other men and be treated like he should have been.

Well, as fate would have it, my two oldest brothers married Teddy's two daughters, and when I was a kid, of course, Teddy was always around. I'd come home one time from up in the woods there with Kenny and Teddy and they'd all stopped to drink on the way home: gonna teach the younger brother the ropes, the fine art of drinking. I suppose we were all pretty well looped by the time we got home.

Kenny brought me home first because I was staying at home and he said, "Smell that, Ma's makin' supper for ya, Bill. Just smell that! It smells like side pork and 'taters and gravy. Teddy, come on in, we'll get Ma to give us something to eat."

Now this is about thirty years later. Teddy said, "Geez, I wouldn't go in that house." He said, "Emily'd shoot me dead as a stone!"

IN BETWEEN THERE SOMEWHERE LIFE GOES ON

In between there, somewhere, life goes on: raising a family, and having fun, and sitting around singing songs and telling stories. That was part of the entertainment.

My mother was content to be a housewife. So many people today don't consider a housewife being a job. It isn't fair. It's a twenty-four hour a day job. That's half the reason there's so many kids committing crimes, because there's too many people working, and not enough of them watching the kids. A lot of the kids is just growing up on their own. And they don't have nothin' to do.

We worked our little backsides off. We started doing chores as soon as you were old enough to know you was a person. If you could communicate with your mother, she was having you do something, if it wasn't any more than going and getting the big spoon out of the drawer so she could mix up a cake. Your reward for being a good boy or good girl and getting that spoon was that you could lick it when she got done.

My mother wrote poetry. She was always singing songs, so people would come around and they'd get entertained. This house right here where we live now was one of the places where they had kitchen hops every weekend. They could have two [square dance] sets in this front room and another set in the kitchen. The big cook stove used to sit out there in the kitchen.

This was written by my mother, Emily B. Smith, in 1965.

51

Occupation—"only a housewife." Oh me, what a dull life indeed!
On the go from dawn to darkness takin' care of my family's needs.
Ten children to wash and cook for, not to mention a hungry man,
Besides all the scrubbin' and cleanin'. Get a kick out of that if you can.
And that was only a small part. I was also counselor and nurse
And planner of menus and grocery lists with an almost empty purse.
There wasn't much time for worry. We just hoped things would turn out all right.
God gave us strength for the day times and the days made us glad for the nights.
But there was always much love and laughter mixed with daily chores
And there was a certain satisfaction in just seein' the freshly scrubbed floors.
Years have passed and now we're just old folks, me and that same hungry man,
In memory we go back together and linger as long as we can.
The hard times have all been forgotten. Only the good times in memory remain.
And if only I could live my life over, I'd be "only a housewife" again.

PART OF THE ORCHESTRA

Over at Cooks Corners, they'd have Pedro [card] parties and square dances. They still have them over at the old schoolhouse. There was that kind of entertainment, but a lot of people made their own. The Laws lived here. They always had kitchen hops and they all played something. They were fiddlers and banjo pickers and guitar players and square dance callers. Every kid in that family had a beautiful voice. There was twelve of them. I think they had two sets of twins. They were brought up in this little house. The mother died young. They would have kitchen hops, and they'd have square dances and box socials at these kitchen hops. Forrest played the fiddle. The boys would sit playing the guitar beside him and the banjo or whatever happened to be in the orchestra that night. Somebody would be standing there calling.

They had a big old cook stove that sat out there in the kitchen. In the summer time, of course, you'd let the stove go out, and it was the bandstand. They'd sit on that old stove and put the oven door down. Forrest Law would sit in the middle, a little short, stocky, bald-headed man. He'd set in the middle, put his feet on the oven door. The oven door had a spring that came out. It would make the door move up and down. When Forrest put his feet on it, he forced the door down and, if he took his feet off, it would rise up a little. And the oven door would become part of the orchestra because it would be going *ee oooo, ee oooo!*—in time with the music. It was wonderful, almost like it was part of the band.

We went by the lighted kerosene lamp. The old round oak stove kept us warm, and the kitchen stove kept us warm at night.

I WASN'T ANY DIFFERENT OF A KID THAN ANY OTHER KID

See, I wasn't any different of a kid than any other kid. You know, when I was a kid I was rebellious. I wouldn't listen. I knew about half of them songs because they were there. You never learned all of them. Now, you can't never learn them or find the words to them or nothin' else!

There's a wonderful song that my mother used to sing. I'd love to find the rest of it. It's called *Traveling* . . . probably an old vaudeville song.

A dozen men once tried pull a mule across the track
They'd pull him just about a foot and then he'd pull
*   em back*
One fella done a funny thing, he musta been a fool
He went and got a piece of straw and tried to tickle
*   the mule.*

And he went Travel-in', travel-in',
Way up in the air, pieces here and there,
But kept travel-in', travel-in',
Far from the old folks at home.

And that was a little chorus that went with it. This young fella had left home because he wanted to go traveling. He left his old daddy and all of his people and he went far, far away. He didn't wait a day, he went traveling. And there was two verses in front of these two. And the last verse was:

At Saratoga once I went to see the ponies race
A man says "Bet on Bumblebee; he's bound win the
*   race"*
So on Bumblebee I set my stake and when the race
*   was won*
I stopped to buzz around a while and I got badly
*   stung,*

So I went travel-in', travel-in',
Back to old New York, I didn't like the walk
But I kept travel-in', travel-in',
Back to the old folks at home.

That's a local "between here and New York City" song.

SO THAT WAS THE BEGINNING OF THAT

Dick Law used to come down to the house all the time. My sister married one of the Law boys. His name was Ivan. They called him "Bug." I guess he liked to play with bugs when he was a kid so they called him "Bug Law." Dick and Bug both sang beautifully. Dick would come down and they would sit around and drink just a little beer. They'd get to singing and they'd sing all night. My mother would sing with them and we'd all sit around there and sing these wonderful old songs: *Ol' Shep* and *Lily Marlene*. Dick, of course, had been in the service so he loved that *Lily Marlene* song. He used to sing it so beautifully. He'd sing *White Cliffs of Dover*—those kind of songs and some of the old Irish songs. Then there was all the tear-jerkers: *Put My Little Shoes Away* and *Baggage Coach Ahead* and all those that they would sit around and sing.

One night Dick had been showing me some things on the guitar, some runs and some things. After Dick left I said to my mother, "You know, if I had a guitar, I bet I could learn to play it."

My mother says, "I bet you could, too. Wouldn't it be nice if you had a guitar? You could learn to play it and we could sit and sing songs at night." I was probably eight or nine years old.

I noticed that a lot of knitting went on. I used to help her sometimes with the knitting. I could do the straight parts of the socks, but I couldn't do the heels or toes or anything. She'd get them going and I would run 'em up there a ways while she'd be starting another one. She knit socks and mittens and sold 'em to the loggers and hunters and people that were in and out.

Just before my birthday come in April, the next spring, the mailman left this triangular box out by

the mailbox. My mother looked out and she said, "You'd better go out and get the mail."

It just happened it came on a weekend. Musta been on a Saturday and I know, because I was home. I wasn't in school. Archie Collins was the mailman, and left that out there. (Maybe Lionel Hepburn was the mailman at that time . . . I can't remember now. They changed right in there.) Well, anyway, I brought that box in and it said *Sears and Roebuck Co.* on it.

My mother said, "You better open that up. That's for you."

I opened it up and there was a little chestnut-colored guitar in there with a covered wagon and a team of oxen on it. There was this cowboy sitting on a horse, riding along side of that. Inside was a book that showed some chords and there was a pick in there.

My mother said, "That's yours for your birthday."

So that was the beginning of that. It was a cheap little guitar and of course it didn't last a whole long time. Four or five years later the plastic knobs on the tuning pegs started to wear out, so I took some metal pieces and soldered them on there but they got to where they slipped off, too. Eventually, I made enough money to buy another guitar, but I learned to play on that little guitar that Ma got me.

We had a battery-operated radio. We'd take the battery out of the car and put it on the radio. Whenever it got staticky, we knew that the battery was getting low. We'd put it back in the car and run the car a while and charge it back up so we could listen to the country music. In the mornings before you went to the barn, you'd turn to WWVA in Wheeling, West Virginia. You could pick that up just like it was in your own back yard. We had a copper aerial that went from that radio out to the barn, all the way from the house to the barn. It'd pick up anything. We could get Nashville, and we could get Cincinnati, Ohio, and all them country stations.

Lee Moore and Wanita would come on in the morning and they would sing and play these pretty runs, these guitar runs, you know. There was a time in there where they was giving sort of lessons. They'd tell you where to put your fingers: "If these young pickers want to learn how to do this, why, we'll show ya. Put your finger here. This finger, the index finger, and your middle finger, and your ring finger and your pinkie. . . ." They'd tell you all these things, "Now strum the guitar." I'd sit there on the edge of the bed and do this and do that, so I learned to play some things. The first thing I learned to play was *Little Home in West Virginia* because that was Lee Moore's theme song. Then came *The Wildwood Flower* and *Jimmy Brown the Newsboy* and some of those things.

THE ROUND OAK STOVE

When my son was but a lad one time I took him
    fishing
In a stream up there not far from our old home.
As we're walking through the woods, I stubbed my
    toe on something
And I found it was the door off Ma's old stove.
So we searched through the ferns and found some
    other pieces.
It sure brought back some memories to me.
'Cause I remembered that old stove, how warm it
    used to keep us,
Carried wood for it till I could scarcely see.

That old round oak stove, it stood there in the parlor
And a big old woodbox sat not far behind,
And almost every evening we all would gather
    round it
When the wind was cold and the snow outside was
    flyin'.

Now Ma got that old stove from the Sisson Lumber
    Company
Back when Pa worked up there in the woods.
They swapped her that old stove and a bunch of
    heavy blankets
For some socks and other hand knit woolen goods.
Now she kept it just like new with that Old Black
    Cat Stove Polish,
And on the top are oak leaves in a circle made of
    chrome.
And on the bottom were chrome rails where we
    used to dry our mittens.
Now it surely added comfort to our home.

That old round oak stove it stood there in the parlor,
And a big old woodbox sat not far behind.

And almost every evening we all would gather
    round it,
When the wind was cold and the snow outside was
    flyin'.

Now I remember when us kids would come in the
    house from playing
And we'd be soaking wet right to the bone.
And Ma would strip us down and we'd all stand
    round in blankets.
Wasn't long till that old stove would have us warm.
Now as I sat there on a log with my son and remi-
    niscing
How that old stove was faithful to the end,
I felt sad but rather happy, as I got to thinkin' bout
    it,
'Cause it was just like meetin' up with some old
    friend.

Oh, that old round oak stove, it stood there in the
    parlor,
And a big old woodbox sat not far behind.
And almost every evening we all would gather
    round it,
When the wind was cold and the snow outside was
    flyin'.
                        —Words and music by Bill Smith—

NOTES

Emily Bicknell Smith must have been one fine, strong mountain woman. Bill's Ma's stories about the Featherbed, and Bill's memories of his own growing-up years, are all true.

Not enough has been written about Emily Bicknell Smith's generation of Adirondack women. Precious exceptions are Edna Teall West's Adirondack Tales: A Girl Grows Up in the Adirondacks in the 1880's *[Willsboro, N.Y.: Adirondack Life, 1970], and Jeanne Robert Foster's* Adirondack Portraits: A Piece of Time, *Noel Riedinger-Johnson, ed. [Syracuse, N.Y.: Syracuse University Press, 1986].*

In her introduction to The Woman in the Mountain: Reconstructions of Self and Land by Adirondack Women Writers, *[Albany, N.Y.: SUNY Press, 1989], Kate H. Winter addresses the issue of limited information about Adirondack women's lives and gives insightful character sketches of the women whose writing is featured in her anthology. A few the pieces are about indigenous woods women. For research that sheds light on why traditional women tell their stories infrequently, see Carol Gilligan's* In a Different Voice: Psychological Theory and Women's Development. *[Cambridge: Harvard University Press, 1982].*

There is a body of fine work about women homesteaders who went west. I particularly like Joanna L. Stratton's Pioneer Women: Voices from the Kansas Frontier, *with an introduction by Arthur M. Schlesinger, Jr. [New York: Simon and Schuster, 1981, and Elinore Pruitt Stewart's* Letters of a Woman Homesteader. *[The Atlantic Monthly Company, 1913. Repriint, Boston: Houghton Mifflin, 1982]*

Interesting as background for looking at 19th and early 20th century American country women are Mary and W. Elliot Brownlee's, Women in the

American Economy,[New Haven: Yale University Press, 1976]; China Galland's Women in the Wilderness [New York: Harper and Row, 1980]; Dorothy Goodfellow's Growing Up Wild [Pacific Grove, CA.: Boxwood Press, 1977]; Roderick Nash's Wilderness and the American Mind [New Haven: Yale University Press, 1967]; Tristram Potter Coffin's The Female Hero in Folklore and Legend [New York: Seabury Press, 1975], and Carolyn G. Heilbrun's Writing a Woman's Life [New York and London: W.W. Norton and Co.,1988].

Barbara Allen and Lynwood Montell's From Memory to History: Using Oral Sources in Local History Research. [Nashville: American Association for State and Local History, 1981] is my favorite resource for thinking about family memories. Allen and Montell explore the structure of memory-based oral narrative, devices for remembering and—most fascinating to me—a chapter they call "Submerged Forms of Historical Truth."

Jan Vansina's Oral Tradition as History [Madison, Wis.: University of Wisconsin Press, 1985] is an approachable analysis of all aspects of the subject. The chapter, "Generations of Messages," and a note on historical gossip are useful tools for thinking about multi-generation family stories.

UNCLE JOHN'S MUSCLE

*All creatures live on opportunity
in a world fraught with disaster.*

—Suzanne Langer—

*We learn by comic instruction
that what seems logical may not be exactly true.*

—Constance Rourke—

MANNERS

In the summertime, a bunch of kids would get appointed to do the milking and whatever. The rest would get appointed to head for the hay field. You tried to get the haying going by the time the dew was off, and then you worked in the hay field until the dew come back on again. That was just about dark,that dusky haze that came just before dark was *dew time.* You headed for the barn with that last load of hay, backed it in, and left it there. You took it off first thing in the morning. That gave any dew that was on it time to dry off before you put it in the mow.

Uncle John used to come around and help during haying time. He was as big a kid as any of the rest of us, always getting into mischief with my father and my mother and causing all kinds of problems. He was a big child is what he was.

My mother, of course, had all kinds of rules and regulations that we had to follow. We had to say "Yes, Ma'm," and "No, Ma'm," and "please," and "thank you," and open the door for anybody that was five minutes older than us. It could get confusing on a Sunday afternoon. There were a lot of people around and we were asking ages to see who you had to open the door for and who you didn't. We didn't want to do anything any more than we had to.

Anyway, this one night we all came marching in up onto the porch after the day's work was done. My mother had three or four wash stands on that porch, wash basins, pitchers and all. You would wash your face and hands and wait in line to go into the house. The youngest would be holding the door for the rest. We'd go strolling through and, "Excuse me," to both the young one and my mother as we went by. We gathered around the table, said grace, sat down to the table and started passing food around.

My mother had another rule. That was that she made two of everything for everybody and that ought to be enough to do 'em. If one person couldn't eat two of something and there was one left—a piece of pie or cake or meat—you could stare at that something all night if you wanted to. You could ask for it, but you weren't going to get it. It got to the point to where you knew better than to ask for it. And you knew better than to reach for it. You never reached across that table. She'd a took your hand off right at your wrist and slapped you right across the face with that bloody hand. So you knew better than to reach out for it.

On this particular night, we had them big old homemade pork chops. We raised our own hogs, so we had lots of good pork chops. We'd kill them when they were about 300 pounds or so. They was good-sized. They was big as steaks, a pork chop from one of them hogs. So there sat this one big pork chop right in the middle of that big meat platter, right in the middle of the table. Every one of us kids was staring at that pork chop, and Uncle John was staring at that pork chop, and our mother was staring at us.

It was dark out. The kerosene lamp was lit right there right next to that meat platter—one of them Aladdin-type lamps—and it was hot in that kitchen. The windows was open, the doors was open, and there wasn't a breath anywhere. All at once a good breeze came up and blew right through that kitchen—*Shhhhh!*—and blew that kerosene lamp right pitch black out.

All you could hear was, "Oh, good God!". It was Uncle John screaming at the top of his lungs. My mother hurried up and got that lamp lit, and there was three forks sticking right out of the back of Uncle John's hand!

So much for the manners when the lights went out.

UNCLE JOHN'S MUSCLE

Uncle John, he used to come to the house all the time. He would come and stay for a week and spend the whole summer. He'd come for another week in the fall and spend the whole winter. Uncle John would be around the house there all the time. My mother would be busy and the kids would be under her feet and everything, with people coming in and coming out. And she's feeding this one and feeding that one.

"John, do something with these kids. They're driving me crazy. Get them out from under my feet. Take them in the other room. Do something with them."

So Uncle John would take us all into the other room. He was a big brute of a man. He'd grab an armful of kids on each side and he'd head for the front room. Kids would be falling out all along the way into the front room. He had these big shoulders and this huge neck and his jaws were wide and his head got narrower as it went up. You've seen those kind of brutey guys. He generally had some kind of a hat setting up on top of that head.

Uncle John had the hairiest chest in the world. Looked like somebody had skinned out a bear and glued the hide right on his chest. He always wore gray undershirts in the summer; they would have been white except that he did his own washing most of the time. And that black hair would shove them undershirts right out there in the front. His hair stuck up out of his chest and come up as far as where he shaved down to this little line around his neck. It kind of curled downward. It looked sort of like a hedge row. It looked like—if somebody took a stick and beat on it—creatures (squirrels, mice and rabbits, such things) might come running out

of there. Might be a good place for a young boy to learn how to hunt or where to hunt, see. . . .

And so he would go in the other room. He'd dump all of us kids on the floor. And he'd say, "Well, what do you want to do? Do you want to hear a story?"

"No, we don't want to hear a story."

"Well, what do you want? Want to hear a song? Let's sing a song."

"No, we don't want to hear no song." And so, "Well, what on earth do you want to do?"

"Well, would you blow your muscle up for us again, Uncle John?"

Well. When you mentioned blowing up his muscle, he would run around the front room three or four times, jump as high as he could. He was really tall, couldn't jump too high because the ceiling was there. He would click his heels together and land back on his feet and show how quick he was. Then he would get down and do about ten or fifteen pushups. Then he would jump up in the air and start flexing his arms back and forth to get primed up so he could blow up his muscle, because, if you blew up a muscle that hadn't been primed up, you could blow the side right out of it. And that would ruin it, see? His muscle'd just have this huge hole there all the while. No one wanted to go around with a hole in the side of their arm like that. He would get everything all flexed and ready to go.

Then he would fling himself down in this big armchair. All the kids would fly into his lap at this point. Uncle John's legs were long enough to where he could hold three kids on each side from his hip to his knees, and another kid on each foot. So he could accommodate eight kids, all at one time. Give them all piggy back rides up and down while he's flexing his arms, getting them in shape to blow his muscle up without punching a hole in it.

Uncle John had a sort of funny-looking thumb, the thumb of a left—handed carpenter is what it was. He would get to pounding with that hammer in that left hand and he'd beat that right thumb so bad that it was about two and a half inches wide and about a half an inch thick. It had turned black one time and just never turned any other color again. The thumbnail was about half way out on it. One day, that thumbnail said, "I ain't taking no more of it. I'm staying right here," and so it never came out any more. He would start getting ready to blow on that thumb to blow up his muscle. He'd flex the thumb a few times, get all set, suck in about ten big deep breaths of air, 'cause it took a lot of air to blow up a muscle this size. He would start blowing. The minute he would start blowing, that muscle would start rising right up. Us kids' eyes would get big, and we'd watch that muscle rise.

He'd get about half way up with that thing and he would stop and hold his hand over the end of his thumb so the air wouldn't come out. Of course, then he would tell you what a brute he was, how he had licked this logger in this camp and this logger in that camp and all this. He would commence blowing again and he would finish blowing that thing all the way up.

When he got through he would hold his hand over his thumb all over again so the air wouldn't come out. And he would say, "Well, who let the air out of this thing last time?"

Nobody'd say a word because they wanted to be first this time.

And then he would say, "Well, was it your mother?"

"No, it wasn't our mother!"

"Well, was it your father?"

"No, it wasn't our father. He's not even here. He's out in the woods."

"Well let's see, was it . . . oh it was, ah, ah, Uncle Jim?"

"No it wasn't Uncle Jim."

And he would go with the whole family all the way down through until he finally got down to whoever's turn it was.

And he'd say, "Well, it must be so and so's turn." Well, so and so, at that point, would lunge at Uncle John's thumb and yank down and give a heck of a yank one way or the other. The air would come—*shhhhhhhhhh!*—right out in your face. And you knew it was coming right out of the end of that thumb, no question about it. But everybody's eyes was staring right at that muscle, and that muscle would drop dead right there in front of you (looked just like a road kill), flatten right out, and sort of lay there like a bowl of jelly.

SHE'S VERY FAMOUS TODAY

Now Uncle John used to drive one of them little square van trucks. He used to go from Potsdam to Syracuse. He'd pick up a load of stuff in Potsdam and deliver it all the way down to Syracuse, to these little stores. And then he would get another load of stuff down in Syracuse and deliver it all the way back to Potsdam. That meant he would spend a couple nights a week in Syracuse. Aunt Lillian was a waitress down there and they kind of fell in love with each other and courted for two or three years before they ended up getting married. She wanted to get away from the city and move up to the country.

Aunt Lillian loved us kids just about to death, and she loved to work in her flower garden, you know. That's another reason she wanted to move to the country. She just loved being out in her flower beds and vegetable gardens. She had a green thumb, Aunt Lillian. She could grow flowers or vegetables right on a rock. There just wasn't anything she couldn't grow. My mother used to take us over there to visit Aunt Lillian on Sunday afternoons.

Oh, she was a hugger and a kisser and all that. Us kids weren't particularly fond of all that kissin' and all that business. She'd be waiting, just lurking back of that window, in that door waiting for us. My mother would pull up into the driveway and pull off the side there with the old car and shut the old car off and *bang!* It would backfire and alert Aunt Lillian that we were there. The kids would all file out into the pathway. You'd see the curtain going in the window, and you knew that Aunt Lillian was waiting, lurking back of that curtain with those kisses just drizzling right off her lips.

The first kid would sneak around to the back of the line when my mother wasn't looking. And the next kid would sneak around the back of the line. And the next kid would sneak around.

Pretty soon my mother would realize that the line was going in the wrong direction, and she would give us one of them famous glares.

The cords in her neck would stick right out. When we saw the cords in my mother's neck we knew that, whatever you're doing, don't do it no more, if you want to live to tell about it. At that point the line would start moving in the forward direction, and there would be Aunt Lillian waiting for the first person to come through that door.

Now Aunt Lillian stood just about four foot six high and just about four foot six wide. Aunt Lillian had the hugest bosoms in the world. Them bosoms broke trail for Aunt Lillian everywhere she went. She could walk through a thousand people, and if they saw her coming, they'd back off and let her walk through there, right down through there. Aunt Lillian had a large rumble seat that stuck out in the back every bit as far as those bosoms did in the front. If she wanted to back up, folks backed out of the way and let her back up as well.

She could part the ways coming or going, Aunt Lillian could.

She loved those flowered house dresses, and polka dots and paisley and all that stuff. She would squiggle herself into them house dresses. When she got everything in there, there wasn't much slack left over. They rode up pretty good in the back there just about two inches just down below that rumble seat, exposing her lily white legs down as far as those rolled-down silk stockings—just above the knees.

Aunt Lillian would be out in them flower gardens working with them short dresses on, picking weeds and digging roots and pulling dirt around the flowers and all that. These old cars, these old square cars would drive up by and *oooga, oooga.* They'd blow their horns and wave and smile. Aunt

Lillian would watch them and smile and wave back to them. Then they'd go up and turn around and come back. By that time she'd be bent over again and they'd toot their horn and wave their hand some more.

And she'd say, "My, John! What friendly folks you have up here on the Featherbed." Innocent old soul.

Well, Aunt Lillian would be waiting behind that door for us kids. The first kid through that door, she was on 'em just like flies on horse manure. She would start right in, "*Mmmmmmm!* My little logger, my little hunter, my little fisherman," whatever you was that day. She would kiss you on the nose, on the eyes, on top of the head, on the ears, anywhere she could land one. She was landing them right on you.

Us kids would stand there, taking deep breaths and sucking in all the air we could get. We looked like Uncle John getting ready to blow his muscle up. She thought we were hyperventilating because we was so excited to see her. The truth of the thing was, we were sucking up air, storing up air because we knew she was going to end all of this with a giant hug. And us kids were just the right height that when Aunt Lillian hugged us, our heads would disappear right in between them huge bosoms, and we didn't breathe again until she let us out of there. When we come out of there, we were kind of blue in the face and we'd go staggering off in the other room.

Poor old Aunt Lillian died before she ever realized she had become a famous person. She's very famous today. You drive around on a Sunday ride out through the country in the fields. You look out in people's back yards and flower gardens and you'll see little wooden statues of Aunt Lillian bent over out there with them polka dot and paisley dresses on, picking them weeds out of that garden.

That's where that came from, from my Aunt Lillian.

BRAVEST TEACHER IN THE WORLD

Back when I was a kid I went to Mrs. Corcoran's old schoolhouse down here. It was during World War II. It was a time. We always figured Mrs. Corcoran was the bravest teacher in the world because everyday she'd have air raid practice. Because the aluminum plants were in Massena, we always figured the Japanese would come and they would bomb Massena and the surrounding villages.

They made airplane parts in Massena. It was a dangerous place to be. Everybody was in the war. All the men folks were gone off to war. My sisters and a lot of other women that I knew worked at that aluminum plant. We always hoped they'd never bomb the plant 'cause we didn't want to lose our loved ones.

Every day Mrs. Corcoran would ring this little bell and she'd holler, "Air raid!" We were afraid that we would look out the window and see them Zeros [Japanese planes] coming across the treetops to blow us to smithereens. When she'd ring that bell, the biggest kid would head for this rug in the middle of the floor and yank that rug back. An old hooked rug it was. Yank that back and underneath there was a little trap door. He'd lift that trap door up out of there and he'd jump down in that old dirt cellar. All us kids would charge into his arms and run and hide in under old desks and things in that little dirt cellar hole. We always thought that Mrs. Corcoran was the bravest teacher in the world, 'cause she never once went down in that hole and hid with us kids. She would stay up there and wait.

She said, "Well, somebody's gotta ring the bell in case something happens. There's gotta be someone to ring the bell to tell you when to come back up." She was terribly brave, that woman.

She would ring the bell after about three or four minutes. The biggest kid would get in under the hole and we'd get in his arms. He'd hoist us up out of the hole, climb back out himself, put the door back, slide the rug back, and we'd all go back to doing our schoolwork, feeling completely safe because we had one of the bravest teachers you could get.

THE AIR SHOW

Now my mother had relatives that were well off. When airplanes came out, I believe they got one or knew someone who had one. Well, my brother Frank got invited to go stay with these more well-to-do relatives, and they took him to the fair.

Well, anyway, my brother saw a man jump out of an airplane with a parachute and he really got excited about it. When he got home he was telling the other brothers, Kenneth and Roswell, about it. Kenneth, the oldest, could make about anything, so they set to work to make one of them parachutes. Kenny would do the sewing. It was up to the others to get the material—old sheets and burlap bags, pieces of blankets and lots of binding twine that was used in hay bales. Well, they worked all week on that parachute. Not a word was said.

It was time for the air show. All the kids stood on the lower side of the house except Frank and Kenny. Now the house was built on the side of a hill, so you could jump from the ground right over onto the woodshed roof. The two boys went up the back of the woodshed and way up onto the roof of the main house and looked over the side. It must have been thirty feet to the ground—or more.

After figuring out the landing spot and placing all the other kids where they wouldn't be in the way, Frank put on the parachute and the two of them went clear to the other end of the house roof. Kenny checked Frank and the parachute to make sure it wouldn't come off, and they were ready.

Frank hollered, "Okay! Here I come!" Kenny held the parachute up in the air and away they went, Frank in the lead and Kenny holding up the parachute so it would be sure and fill up with air.

81

When Frank reached the end of the roof he leaped with both hands out in front and both legs spread so he could glide softly to the ground. When Kenny came to the end of the roof, he stopped and threw the parachute into the air.

Well, that parachute probably weighed three times what Frank did. The two headed for the ground—side by side! When Frank saw that parachute gliding along beside him, he was sort of disappointed. When they hit the ground, Frank's knees hit him in the chin, and that's all he could remember.

When he could remember, Ma and Pa and old Doc Swartz were standing by the side of Frank's bed.

When Frank finally got them in focus, he said "It never even opened."

I don't think there were any more air shows at our house.

SIGN OF THE FLYING RED HORSE

Now Roswell, my brother Roswell, used to drive a log truck. Did you ever hear of Vinny Kavanaugh up in Tupper Lake, Kavanaugh Trucking? My brother and Vinny used to drive together. Eventually Vinny started his own trucking company, but my brother just drove truck.

He used to take me with him when I was a little kid. I loved to go with Roswell in that log truck. Had an old broken baby carriage. Wheels on them old baby carriages had little spokes in them, just like a wagon wheel, and that axle was intact for that one wheel. Now there was a hole in the dash of that truck. Used to stick that axle in that hole. Used to be some kind of a meter or something in here. I could sit in that truck and with that axle stuck through that hole, pull down on that and it held it right in there. I could steer with that wagon wheel. It was my steering wheel. I would make noises—*brrrrrm, brrrrrrrm!* And I could drive that log truck. While my brother was driving on the other side, I could drive it on this side.

One time we went up and got a load of logs up in Tupper Lake. He was heading down for Sissin's Mill in Potsdam with that load of logs. We got pert near into Colton, and BANG! One of them tires blew on that log truck. The old truck swayed back and forth. My brother pulled it off the side of the road there and got out and looked to see what tire it was, and he said, "Well it's one of them tires on the back on the dummy there, and when we get up to Ernie Bancroft's gas station, why, we'll fix it."

Ernie Bancroft owned the big gas station up on top the hill. It was one of them "flying red horse" gas stations, and it was red and white. You pulled up there. You couldn't pull in because there was this long awning that came out in front of that gas station with posts out there, and these pumps, these gas pumps, were setting under that awning not too far from them posts. They had glass balls up on the top and the flying red horse on there. When you cranked—they didn't have the electric yet; they still had the old crank ones—when you cranked that, the gas would go around inside this little ball. There were some little things inside that looked like little dice, and they would bounce around in there. That bubble-bubble gas would go around. All these bubbles and them little things going around fascinated a little kid when he'd watch all that. On this post that stuck out on the end of that awning hung down this big metal sign, and it squeaked, sounded like it should be oiled. It was a sign of the flying red horse. There was a big red Pegasus on that sign, and it would sway back and forth in the breeze.

Ernie Bancroft liked me, because he said I was one of the few young lads that knew enough to go in his store and keep his hands in his pockets and not touch anything. Besides that, I knew how to shoot a gun. Ernie Bancroft was a crack shot and a gunsmith. He'd let me shoot his guns when I'd go down there.

My brother took the spare tire off the top of the log truck, threw it down on the ground and said, "There, set down on that tire and I'll get you an Orange Crush."

Well, he went in to get me an Orange Crush and Ernie says, "Who's that for? Billy?"

And my brother said, "Yeah."

"Well," he said, "There ain't no charge for that Orange Crush. You give that to Billy. I always give Billy an Orange Crush when he comes 'cause he's a good boy." And Ernie came out and patted me on the head and gave me the Orange Crush. He told me I was a good boy, so I sat on that spare tire while my brother was jacking up the truck and taking that off.

Now an Orange Crush was a lot bigger in those days than they are today. There was a lot of soft drink in one of them for a little feller. While I'm sitting there watching my brother jack up the truck, this big car pulled in to that yard, and this city dude got out of that car. You knew that he was some kind of a salesman or something, and he looked quite well off. He had on this sort of a blue suit, and that suit had creases right down the front of them legs. Couldn't imagine what anybody'd have to have a suit pressed quite that much for. Then he had on this white belt that went around there and held on them blue pants, and this kind of striped blue shirt inside. He had a little vest on there. It was kind of open in the front. He had a tie on, and right in the middle of that necktie was a little pin that held that right there to his shirt. I'm watching all this, and I'm looking up and down. I looked down there, and there I saw the first pair of white shoes that I ever saw in my life, those white suede shoes. He opened that back door up. He reached in the back of that car and he took out this real fancy hat. I'd never seen a hat like this before. It was the first Panama hat that I'd ever seen. It had little circles in the side. It looked like it might be made out of fresh straw or something, and it was kind of cream-colored. And there was little dots, little holes in that hat, little ventilation holes, I suppose. He put that hat on there, and he looked back in that window of that car and set that hat just so on his head. You could tell he was a businessman. He reached in the back of that car and he took out this little suitcase—now a days I guess they call it a briefcase, and he went on in there to Ernie's store.

Well, I'd taken all that in. I'd watched my brother with a jack and all and he was about ready to change that tire. That Orange Crush had started taking its toll on this little boy.

I said, "Roswell, I got to go pee, Roswell."

And so Roswell said, "Okay, just a minute." And

85

he finished jacking up there and locked the jack so it wouldn't go anywhere.

I said, "Hurry up, Roswell, I really got to go pee real bad." So he took me, and we headed out back.

Ernie Bancroft had the biggest privy in the world. He always figured, I guess, he was going to get a lot of business someday, because there was about a seven holer out there. And way down at the far end was a little boy's hole. It had a soft drink case turned bottom side up standing there in front of it so that little boys could reach. And because little boys weren't particularly good shots, why he had a piece of a two gallon oil can that they used to make out of metal back in them days. They weren't plastic. He had cut that out with a pair of tin sheers, and he'd nailed it up on the back there for a splash board. *Right in the center of that was one of them flying red horses!* If you could hit that red horse, things were going to work pretty good for you and you weren't going to miss at all.

We hunted around there for a minute and finally found what we was looking for. I started going in the privy there, and all at once that city dude come right in to that privy, right over on the far end over there, that big sittin' hole on the end there. I figured he probably was going to sit down over there. He checked it out pretty good. He reached in his shirt pocket and slipped his vest back there. He took out something I'd never seen before: nowdays they call them a Kleenex. He took that little piece of paper and he wiped that seat all off around there. Then he got some more of that paper out of his pocket and he started lining around that seat with that paper. He reached in—to get another piece of that paper I suppose—and when he did, a five dollar bill that was folded up in his pocket fell out of there and it *chuuu, chuuuuuu, chuuuu!*— right down that hole. Well, that guy stood there for a good minute and a half and he looked down that hole at that five dollar bill and finally he reached in his back pocket and he pulled out that billfold and opened it up and took out a fifty dollar bill out of that billfold. If you looked you could see right on it. It said "fifty dollars" right on it. He dropped that fifty dollar bill right down that hole, and he put that billfold right back in his back pocket.

My brother let a scream right out of him that would curdle your blood. "Good grief, man, don't you know that's a fifty dollar bill?"

He said, "Yes I know that's a fifty dollar bill. You don't think I'm going to climb down in there for a lousy *five* dollars, do you?"

FIXING THE PIG FENCE

My father used to work in the logging camps. He would be home on the weekends. About every two or three weeks he'd come home for a weekend. Whenever he left, he always left me with plenty of chores to do. He'd write out stuff on paper and leave it for me. I'd have to have that done when he got back. That's all there was to it.

I knew that he was home, and I knew that him and my mother were sitting in the front room reading the newspaper. I thought," If I could just sneak up them stairs, maybe he'll forget to give me all the orders that I know he's gonna give me. And he'll go back to the camp and forget about it."

I took my sneakers off. I had them in my hand and I slipped up the stairs and got pretty near to the top step. And I heard. "Bill, come on down here a minute. I got a bunch of stuff I got to talk to you about. There's a lot of things I want you to do while I'm gone."

So I come down.

He said, "You know, we just ordered fifteen new pigs. They're going to be coming in a couple weeks. By the time I get back, why they'll be ready. I just got some new chicken wire and some new staples.

I want you to tear the old chicken wire out of that pig fence down there and dig it up and make a trough around there. Dig a trench around there and put the new wire in and nail it up tight and bury it back up so the pigs can't get out. You know they'll root right under that fence under them logs."

Now our pig fence looked like a corral. It was made out of logs. It looked like a short log cabin, about four foot high. In the corner of that was a little shack, built in there for the pigs to get under.

There was always hay kept in there. The pigs would go out into that pig yard, and they would come back in under that little shack. That's where their clean spot was. The rest was all muck. I took that wheelbarrow and that roll of brand new chicken wire and the staples. I stuck the hammer in my back pocket, and I went on down there. It was in the spring of the year and the blackflies and mosquitoes were as thick as hair on a dog. I shoveled a ditch down to the bottom of that fence. I was pulling that old wire out and rolling it up. I would put the new wire in and unroll it as I went. I figured when I was done I wouldn't have to go back through that muck, wallowing in it. I could just fill it in as I went along and I'd have it all done. When I got done, I would be completely done. That's what I was doing, working my way all the way around that corral.

All at once I could hear, *rrrrrrrrr, rrrrrrrrr, rrrrrr!* I looked up on that hill and I thought sure I was gonna see Zeros coming right over the top of that hill. The Japanese were going to come, and they were gonna bomb us for sure. I looked up there, and you know what I saw? I didn't see Zeros. I saw the biggest giant mosquitoes that I ever saw in my life!

Those things was big as wild turkeys. They was coming over that hill with them eight-to-ten-inch beaks stuck right out straight in front of them there, coming right at me just as fast as they could come. *Rrrrrr, rrrrrrrrr, rrrrrrrrrr!*

Boy, I headed for that house hollerin', "MA!" at the top of my lungs. I was boggin' up through there, and those things were gaining on me something fierce. I realized I wasn't going to make it to that house. There wasn't any place to go. There was no out buildings or nothin' there. All there was was that big old hog kittle turned bottom side up.

Well, a hog kittle is an iron kittle that folks used to use for butchering purposes. It's made out of cast iron. If you left it right side up it would fill up with rain water, and that water would freeze. Because ice expands, it would break that iron kittle, bust it wide open. We always kept it upside down on about three or four little stones. They'd sink in the ground and it would sit there. It wouldn't work its way down in the ground because it was sitting on them stones. You could pick it up when you're ready because it was just sitting there. Well, I headed for that kittle. Now that kittle weighed pert-near two hundred pounds. I reached down there to yank that up to hide underneath there.

You think that I could pick that thing up?

No, I couldn't pick that thing up.

Just then one of them mosquitoes prodded me right in that red patch in the back of my overalls. Well, I'm telling you I found some strength I didn't know I had! I picked that thing up. I dove underneath that thing, and that kittle come crashing down. It was pitch black dark under there.

"There. you guys! That'll fix you. You can't get me now." I could hear them, *rrrrrrr, rrrrrrrrrr, rrrrrrrrrrr,* and a buzzing around that kittle. And pretty soon I could hear walking. They were galloping all over on top of that kittle. *Pitter-patter, pitter-patter on top of that kittle.*

I thought, "Go ahead. Wander around on there all you want. But you're not going to get me underneath this iron kittle."

And all at once I heard, **drrrrrrr! Tut,tut,tut!** It sounded like a little miniature jack hammer. I looked up, and a ray of light come right through that kittle. They had drilled a hole right through that kittle. And this one guy stuck his beak right down through, and he started looking all over for me under there. Pretty soon *drrrrrrrr! Tut,tut,tut!* Another ray of light and another beak come down through. *Drrrrrrrr! Tut,tut,tut!* Another ray of light and another beak. Beaks are going all around under there. Looked like long stiff strings of spaghetti looking for me. Pretty soon, *drrrrrr!*

tut,tut,tut!—another ray of light. I got pretty worried there.

I was kind of digging my way down into China as far as I could dig with my hands. I was saying prayers that hadn't been invented yet.

All at once I realized that I had that hammer in my back pocket. I said, "I'll fix them guys." Well I took that hammer out of my back pocket, and I started bending over them beaks. *Tunk, Tunk, tunk*—I'd bend them right over just like you'd bend over an old rusty nail. I said, "There, that'll hold that guy." and *Tunk, tunk, tunk*—bend it right over. Boy, I'm having fun, bending over all these beaks! *Tunk, tunk, tunk*—left hand, right hand. I'm having a great time. I was having so much fun I wasn't paying attention. *Drrrrrr! tut,tut, tut!* Another ray of light, and another beak. *Drrrrrr! tut,tut,tut!* Another ray of light, and another beak. *Tunk, tunk, tunk*—and pretty soon there was so many mosquitoes clinkin' there that that hog kittle started wavering.

They picked that two hundred pound hog kittle up and flew right over the trees with it and went right out of sight off into the woods there. I headed for the house just as fast as I could go. "Ma!" I'm hollering. Well, you know there was two of them mosquitoes left and they swooped down there, *Drrrrrrrrr, rrrrrrrrrrr!* And they started circling around me. One of them grabbed me right by that red patch on the seat of my overhalls. The other one grabbed me right by the nap of the neck and them gallusses and picked me right up off the ground. Well, I'm running and hollering, and my feet was still going. I looked down. I must have been thirty foot off the ground and I was still trying to run—but I wasn't going anywhere, only up.

Well, them mosquitoes got in an argument. The one that had a hold of the seat of my britches was hauling me off to the left. And the one had a hold of me by the back of my neck was hauling me off to the right. And one says, "Let's take him down to the swamp and eat him."

And the other says, "No, if we take him down to the swamp to eat him the big ones will take him away from us. Let's take him up here in the woods and eat him."

They were pullin' and hauling back and forth there. And I was hoping for the one that was headed for the woods, 'cause I didn't want to see none of them big ones. All at once the one that was headed for the swamp lost hold. That patch let go from the seat of them britches and that mosquito slammed up against the side of a big pine tree. The last I saw of him there was big *x's* in his eyes going right down, end over end through them limbs. And I guess he was a goner.

When that happened I swung down like a pendulum on a clock, and that mosquito that had a hold of the back of my shirt and them galluses lost hold of my shirt. All he had a hold of was them stretchy old galluses. I started to fall and them galluses started to stretch. I almost touched the ground with my feet and them galluses would pull me right back up again.

Down I'd go and back up I'd go, and down and run some more.

Back up I'd go.

Pretty soon the buttons started to fly off my pants that was holding them gallusses. Now we didn't always have them metal things that we have today that don't work, you know. We used to have buttons on there with a leather thong that held them right on there. And they worked pretty good. Well, they couldn't take all that pressure, though, and the buttons started popping off them pants— *bing, bing, bing, bing, bing!* Them gallusses went up into the air. They wrapped around that mosquito and killed him cold stone dead. He started for the ground, end over end over end over end, and I started for the ground end over end over end. And all at once, *crrrrrrash!*

I thought, "Well, I guess I'm dead."

Then I heard, "Bill! Bill, will you wake up ?" It was my mother.

The room was a mess. The feathers was all over the room. I caught my toe in the feather tick and ripped a big chunk out of it. Ripped my pillow. There was feathers from that all over. Tipped over my drinking glass of water that was on the floor. Water mixed with the feathers. Tipped over the kerosene lamp. The room was a mess.

And she said, "Good Lord, Bill, you musta had a horrible nightmare! You pick up this room and get it all nice and cleaned up. And get yourself dressed and washed up and everything. Come down and have breakfast.

"And don't you forget: when you get done having breakfast you've got to go down and fix that hog fence for your father today."

HAY MAKERS' SWITCHEL
[cold drink]

1 cup brown sugar
1/2 tsp. ginger
1/2 cup molasses (optional) or white sugar
3/4 cup vinegar
2 quarts cold water

Mix well.

NOTES

With the exception of "The Air Show," a true Featherbed story, and "The Bravest Teacher in the World," the tales in Uncle John's Muscle are Bill's own memories—turning the corner into traditional tall tales and travelling jokes.

"She's Very Famous Today" is Bill Smith in his most brilliant simpleton disguise, building details until they explode into—shall we say—something more than the sum of its parts. "The Sign of the Flying Red Horse" is the most concrete, brilliant build-up to a migrant numskull motif I've ever seen. "Fixing the Pig Fence" uses the frame story [a story within a story] device to get us to that great telling of the giant mosquitos and the kettle. Variants of the giant insect story have been reported in American traveller's yarns and almanacs since the 18th century, and in European magic tales before that.

Constance Rourke's American Humor: A Study of the National Character [1931] has been reprinted with introduction and bibliographic essay by W.T. Lhamon, Jr. [Tallahassee: University of Florida Press, 1986]. Rourke, well ahead of her time in looking at art in a cultural and historic context, traces the origin and development of key American comic stereotypes [the Yankee, the backwoodsman, the peddler, and the minstrel] through American history, literature, and folklore. Her work shows us where the folks on the Featherbed got their tales and their local versions of American "stock characters."

Other good books about American humor are Walter Blair's Horse Sense in American Humor from Benjamin Franklin to Ogden Nash [Chicago: University of Chicago Press, 1942]; Richard M. Dorson's Man and Beast in Comic Legend [Bloomington, Ind.: University of Indiana Press, 1982]; W. Howland Kenny's Laughter in the Wilderness: Early American Humor to 1783. [Kent, Ohio: Kent State University Press, 1973], and Louis D. Rubin's The Comic Imagination in American

Literature. *[New Brunswick, N.J.: Rutgers University Press, 1973].*

Several articles in Folklore, Cultural Performances, and Popular Entertainments: A Communications-Centered Handbook, *edited by Richard Bauman [New York and Oxford: Oxford University Press, 1992], shed light on the world of Bill's stories:* Oral Culture *by Jack Goody;* Humor; *by Mahadev L. Apte;* Ethnography of Speaking, *by Joel Sherzer;* Oral History, *by Trevor Lummis, and* Tourism., *by Barbara Kirshenblatt-Gimblett and Edward M. Bruner. In his introduction, Bauman observes that the ". . . .communicative forms and practices of a society—its way of speaking, dressing dancing, playing music, and so on—are social means that are available to members for the accomplishment of social ends." In addressing what he calls the "commodification of culture," Bauman warns, " . . . folklore also tends to romanticize and idealize traditional peoples and social formations . . . this makes the term suspect in the eyes of those who see folklore as anachronistic and the romanticization of dominated peoples as itself an instrument of domination."*

Adirondack woods guides, romantic but certainly not dominated, make their livings from the "commodification of culture," and—to some extent—from marketing themselves *to city people. The introduction to* I Always Tell the Truth (Even If I Have to Lie to Do It), *Vaughn Ward, ed. [Greenfield Center, NY: Greenfield Review Press, 1990] describes the social context for the excange of North Country tales, the process of formulaic learning in oral cultures, and the function of humorous, covert verbal competitions in a relatively closed society.*

SNOW CULVERTS

The world stands on absurdity.
and perhaps nothing would have come to pass without it.

—Fyodor Dostoevsky, The Brothers Karamazov—

The comic comes into being just when society and the
individual, freed from the worry of self-preservation,
begin to regard themselves as works of art.

—Henri Bergson, *Laughter*—

EARL PHILLIPS

Earl Phillips was one of the nicest old fellows that ever was. Earl always wore lots of patches on his pants, lots of patches on the elbows of his old frocks. He'd wear them old green and black Malone (now they're Woolrich but back in them days they were Malone) frocks. The knees would all be out of the pants. They'd be patched four, five times— patch on top of the patches.

When the kids at school in Colton used to make fun of my patches, I used to think of Earl. I knew it wouldn't have bothered him, so I felt I was a better person for remembering Earl. Besides, my mother said there was nothing wrong with patches as long as you were clean and not to worry about those stuck-up kids. Earl always wore an old cap of some kind. The cardboard would stick out the front of the thing and be all crumpled up. The cloth kind of hung down there in front.

He didn't really wear whiskers. He was just one of these guys who didn't shave much, so he'd have all this white stubble all over his face. It would get as long as a half inch, sometimes, or an inch sometimes. He had sort of a large nose. He had an interesting, well-lined face. He was a nice old guy.

I had first met Earl through my neighbor, Chet Boice, who was a nephew of Earl's. "Uncle Earl," Chet called him. Chet took me all over the place. Earl was a gunsmith and a fix-it-all. There wasn't anything Earl couldn't fix. Jack-of-all-trades he was. He could do anything. He could make some of the nicest guns you ever saw. He would go out on the stone walls and he would go along and find these old buggies and all these old broken things that had been thrown on the stone wall. He loved to find an old buggy axle because the iron in them axles made good steel for a gun barrel. He would take that buggy axle back, he'd get out his little forge and start hammering away on that thing. He had these special drills and all that stuff. He'd take a little piece of thread and run it down the side of that and he would line that right up and the next thing you know he had made an octagon barrel for a gun and it would be true as anything in the world. Then he would ream that out with his long rod with a drill on the end of it and drill that all out and crank that thing. He had his forge there. He'd heat everything just the right color when he hammered it. He had these guns around all the time. A bunch of us kids were going by there one day on our bicycles. We were going somewhere and Earl was outside, so we all had to stop and visit with Earl.

It was one of them summers. It had rained all summer long. It just was really a bad summer. Nobody's crops were any good. Nothing was growing. It just was awful. Earl, of course, saw us go by and we stopped, and when he waved to us, why we pulled right in and had to go visit with him.

"Made any new guns lately, Earl?"

"Oh, yeah, I got a good one in there. You want to try it? Give it a try if you want to. I'll bring it out."

He brought it out. He took an old wash tub that Maud had around there full of holes. There was a pole stuck out on the end of his little shop, out there where he'd hang a deer, or hog or whatever. It was a hanging pole. He hung that tub off the end of that pole, if I remember right. We all started shooting at the center of that tub. He took a piece of charcoal and he drew an X in the middle of that tub. We were shooting at the center of that X and almost going right through the same hole every time. That gun shot perfect.

All at once we could hear an airplane coming. Earl took the gun right out of the kid's hand, whoever had it, and leaned it up against the side of the chicken coop there and he looked up at the sky and he looked up at that airplane. Us kids looked at Earl, and we looked at that plane and we looked at Earl and those white whiskers, and looked up.

Earl had sort of large holes in his nose and the white hair come out those holes. We were looking up at Earl—at his nose. His face and his eyebrows stuck out quite far. They looked like a little porch, sitting out over top of the whole thing here, as we were looking up at this wonderful man. He had his hands in them pants pockets and he's watching that airplane all the way across the sky. It disappeared out of sight over on the other side of the sky.

He turned to us kids and he said, "No wonder it's rained all summer long. Them air wagons driving right through them clouds, busting them clouds all up. That's why it's rained all summer long. Darn air wagons!"

Those old timers, they had a reason for everything.

THEM FELLERS FROM ROD CHESTER

Old Lanty Martin, he lived there in Cooks Corners. Lanty, of course, he was another hound man. He had black and tans, redbones, blueticks and all kinds. They had interbred so much that they were just hounds. They weren't anything. They were just Lanty Martin's hounds.

Old Lanty, he'd be up in the woods there somewhere hunting them foxes. Lanty kind of walked sort of sideways. I don't know if he'd hurt his hip sometime or other, or what—in a loggin' accident or something. He dragged one leg, sort of, and come down the road sideways.

You'd look up the road and see him coming sideways down the road, all them hounds coming sideways down the road, cocking up at every bush and briar along the way. You'd cock your head 'cause it looked like the whole world had just flipped over a little bit.

He'd come down to the general store and he'd have his old shot gun. He used it for a cane. The butt plate was wore right off it. It was all round on the bottom, rubbing on them cobblestones all the while. Everybody marveled at the fact that he hadn't blowed his brains out with that thing pointed at his head all the time. He'd come up on the porch of the store there and set his pack basket down and us kids would be sitting around there.

"Boy, see that gun there?"

"Yup"

"Don't you dare touch that gun. It's loaded. It'll kill you."

We knew that we weren't supposed to touch a gun anyway.

One of his favorite stories was how he got rid of them fellers from Rochester. He'd say, "Have I told you that story lately?"

We'd say, "No." (He hadn't told us since he left that morning.) And so he would tell us his story.

Now all these old people around here were guides and would take people out hunting. These slickers, or these sports, they'd pay you pretty near to death. When they come to your place, why, they'd pay you for putting them up, and they'd pay you for feeding them and they'd pay you if they got a deer, they'd pay you for that. If they couldn't hit one and you'd get it for them, then they'd pay you for that.

It was fine for about four or five years.

Then something happened.

You became friends. Once you became friends, they didn't pay you no more. Now these fellows had been coming to Lanty's for quite a few years and they hadn't paid him in about five or six years. He was getting pretty sick of them fellers from "Rod chester," as Lanty called it.

Well, this one time they pulled in right in the middle of the night.

"Lanty, take us out huntin' in the morning."

So he went out with that game leg, going all through the woods, chasing deer to these guys and all. 'Course he'd set them right in the middle of a deer trail. He'd get sick of them missing.

You'd say, "One of them's gonna die when that deer comes over that hill; he's either going to shoot the deer for self protection or he's gonna get run over, one or the other."

You'd plunk them here and plunk them there and plunk them there. You wouldn't hear a shot fired—with tails going all over the place. Nobody's shooting nothing.

Old Lanty had put in an awful long day. He was getting real sick of these fellers. So they got back that night. They grabbed the last beer out of the spring there and went into the house. They were drinking that last bottle of beer and never offered any to Lanty or anything, sitting around. Lanty made them a great big old venson supper, early venson. Everybody had some early venson. That was a deer that met his doom along in August or so and got cut up and put into jars and put in the spring out in the hillside somewhere. He had fixed them this nice supper of venson and potatoes and gravy and the whole business. When they got all through, they all headed for the other room in there, to drink that last beer.

Old Lanty says, "Wish somebody'd come out here and help with these dishes."

Nobody paid any attention to him at all, as if he wasn't even there.

"By Golly, I wish somebody'd come out and help with these dishes. Lot of dishes to do out here, you know."

Nobody paid no attention. They were telling deer stories. If they'd a been where they were supposed to been they'd a got a big buck, and all that stuff.

Lanty didn't want to hear none of that. He already knew that. He says, "Well, then, I suppose I gotta do these dishes just like I always do them."

He goes out to the back door and he hollers, "Here Blue! Here Sue! Here Red! "

All them old big hounds come bouncing into that kitchen sideways, ears a-floppin', tails a-waggin'. Lanty goes over the table and he throws them plates down on the floor. And them hound dogs, they rattled them old tin plates down there, licked off them places where the porcelain chunks were taken out. They polished them all up slick as a hound's tooth, so to say.

Lanty says, "You boys do the nicest job on them dishes. By gosh, never seen nothing like it."

Then he goes and he gets them cups. He throws them down there on the floor. They rattled them cups all around, got down into the bottom of them cups, pulled out them fortunes and tea grounds, and polished them all up slick as you please.

Lanty just marveled all the way through the whole thing, saying "By gosh, what good jobs them dogs' doing on these dishes."

He went and got the silverware. He threw that

down on top of everything. They rattled that all over, that genuine stainless steel silverware of his. They got right in between the tines on the forks, and polished everything all up in good shape.

Then comes the time that they're done. Everything's clean and you got to get those half-fed hounds outdoors. Now that's not an easy chore, 'cause anybody who would feed a hound at supper time is crazy. They're going to be hungry long about three in the morning, and start bellering all night. You always waited to just before you went to bed to feed them hound dogs. I don't know if you ever tried to get a half- fed hound out the door or not, but they got a lot of hide on them. Grab them by the nap of the neck and they brace them great big feet and they don't go nowhere. You walk about five foot before you ever come to that dog. Finally the dog will start moving. You get him to the door and he braces them feet against that door and you got to run out there about five feet, get him started, sneak by him, and give him a kick in the rump all at the same time. That's not an easy chore to get him out the door, see. Well, he went through that with about half a dozen of them hounds and finally got them out doors.

All the while he's marveling at what a great job them dogs do on them dishes. By gosh, they're polished right up slick and clean. He went and got them plates and he opened up that cupboard and he started putting them plates right up there where the plates went. He closed the cupboard door and he come back just in a-marveling again and he picked up all the silverware and he opened up the drawer and he threw all the forks in where the forks go, and the knives and the spoons in their place.

These fellers are starting to pay attention there now. They're looking out through that door in the front room and they're watching Lanty put them dishes away and then he goes and gets them cups, old Lanty, hangs them up underneath them cup hooks underneath them cupboards. Marvels at the wonderful job the dogs did.

Finally, the guy that was in charge of them fellers from Rodchester, he says, "Ya know, Lanty, Joe, that new fella that we brought up this year for the first time? He's got a wicked pain in his right side and we're afraid he might have appendicitis. We think we better get him back to Rochester before that thing busts."

They loaded poor old Joe into their big car and headed off for Rochester, never to be seen again.

And that's how Lanty got rid of them fellers from Rod chester.

HOW DO YOU GET TO POTSDAM

Lanty was going down the road with all of his hounds one day, lookin' to see if anything had crossed the road he could sick them hounds on. He'd have it back in the shed by dark if there was. Folks that were rich went to Clarkson, Potsdam State, St. Lawrence University, the Aggie School in Canton. They'd look at a map and they weren't long figuring out that you had to go clear around by Lake George to get up in this country or clean around by Utica to get up in this country. That was a long haul around there, but if you looked at the map and you saw those little gray lines you could see that there was county roads that went right up through into the North Country. And you could follow them county roads. You *might* not get lost. Who knew?

Well, by the time them people got to Cook's Corners, they was stone dead lost, sort of afraid, and didn't know just what to expect of life ever again.

Well, Lanty, he's going down the road with all them hounds. This great big black car pulled right up beside of him, and there's this little guy sitting in the back of that car with the little beanie on his head. You knew they were headed for Clarkson University in Potsdam. Nobody 'round here had much and when you saw somebody with a big car like that, you were a little jealous. You had to be a little jealous, you know, if you were human at all.

Now that woman was rather rude. She yanked the window right down there, and she hollered out there, "*Hey, old man!* How do you get to Potsdam?"

Well, Lanty never did anything fast in his life. He had a cud of tobacco in his cheek about the size of a softball. He yanked that thing out, flung it over there in the woods, and all them hounds pounced onto that cud, and started ripping it apart. They liked chewing tobacco, too. They were snarling and growling and biting each other on the ears.

That woman's got big eyes and she's cranking the window up there.

Lanty had about two and a half inches of white whiskers there with a brown tobacco juice stain right down the center of them whiskers and right down the front of them bib overhauls that he had on. That overhall jacket and that blue work shirt had tobacco juice on it, too. He had them little brown teeth; he chewed tobacco since he was about three, you know. He'd wore them teeth right off. The only complexion them teeth had that showed any white at all was where the nerves stuck out on the ends there where he chewed them right off.

He reached in his back pocket there and he pulled out that paper of Beechnut Tobacco. He opened it up. He fed a brand new chew into that cheek and got that cheek back up off his shoulder again there because he took the slack out of it. Rolled that paper back up and rolled that tobacco round in his mouth there a few times. Kinda chewed it a little bit and did it up a little the way he wanted it.

Stuck that paper back in his back pocket, leaned against the side of that car.

And he said, "Well. . . ., generally my sister takes me."

MUD SEASON

My father was working up in the logging camp skidding with the horses. He wouldn't work his horses in the mud in the spring because they might get hurt. This one time my father figured that mud season would be right in full tilt by the end of the week and it would be time to come out of the woods. He got surprised about Monday or Tuesday when it started raining. The mud season came a little early, and by the weekend, it was in full bloom. He started out of the woods. He started sinking in the mud and had to take the horses back. He couldn't bring them out, so he left them there with the chore boy.

He decided that whatever would work on the snow ought to work on the mud, so he went looking around and he found the longest pair of snowshoes he could find. He put on them snow shoes. They went right along on top of that mud just dandy. He stayed right up on the top, so he started for home. He walked about ten miles out of the woods on top of that mud—all the way down through that old tote road, got up on the hill above our house and started down around the bend and then got down on the flat. Just before he got to our place, he saw this hat laying there in the mud.

He said, "Jeeze, that looks like Will Newton's hat. It musta blowed up the road here, wind musta blowed it up. I'll take it in the house and Emmy'll wash it up. I'll take it down to Will when things dry out a little bit." Will Newton lived just down the road.

So he reached down and picked that hat up and there was Will's head under that hat.

My father said, "Will, you're in trouble ain't ye?"

Will says "I guess *I'm* all right, but I'm not so sure 'bout this horse I'm sittin' on."

MORRIS RIVERS

Morris Rivers lived up over there in the woods and him and his wife Emma lived by themselves. Emma had been a school teacher and retired. She and Morris had a few dollars they'd saved up through the years.

They bought a tractor. Morris was up working with the tractor one day on a hot August afternoon when it broke. So he took a wrench and took the part off and headed for home.

Morris had some relatives up in that country that had moved years ago to Florida and had made quite a lot of money. They come back up every summer to visit. They had a little house up above there where they came. They would stay up there for two or three weeks in the summer. They happened to be going to Canton for some reason or other, that particular day, and they had their black Florida car with air-conditioning in it. It was deathly hot, one of those real still days.

Now Morris was walking down the road with that broken part in his hand and these relatives stopped to give him a ride. He got in the back seat of the car. Morris had his sleeves all rolled up and his shirt opened. He was fanning himself with his straw hat. It was hot. Morris always cleared his throat, "Eh, *Eh*," before he spoke.

And so, "Eh, *Eh*."

"Good day ain't it?"

"Yup"

"What're you doing Morris?"

"Well I was up there working in the field and a part broke on the tractor so I figured I'd have to go down to Canton and get me a new part for it."

They visited and talked for a while. The air-conditioning was on in that car. Morris started buttoning up his collar, roll down his sleeves and he buttoned his sleeves. Pulled down his hat down over his ears.

One of them spoke and said, "Morris, you going back up there and put that part back on that tractor this afternoon and finish that mowing back there?"

Morris said, "Well, you know I was going to, but it's turned so cold here that I believe I'll go back home and kill a hog."

SNOW CULVERTS

Well, this was a real bad winter and so I sat here in the front room looking out the window for the first five or six weeks and watched it snow. And then, for the next five or six weeks, I sat in the upstairs window and watched it snow. The next five or six weeks of winter, I sat in the attic and watched it snow. We had these huge snow banks. You'd open the door and there was this big wall of snow. As luck would have it, I was smart enough to always have my snow shovel inside the house, so whenever you opened the door, why you could start right out shoveling.

I had to dig tunnels out to the garage, tunnels out to the barn, tunnels out to the wood pile, and everything. Then, of course, long about February, I run out of wood. I had to dig another tunnel all the way up to the wood lot. That was kind of hard because every twenty-five or thirty feet you had to dig an *up* tunnel to throw the snow out, which came in handy. Once I got the main tunnel dug out there. I had to go get the wood with the tractor, why the exhaust fumes went right up through them holes. I didn't get asphyxiated or anything. It worked just fine, so I went over there and started cutting down a bunch of trees.

Well, when you got twenty foot of snow, there ain't no such thing as cutting *down* a tree. You just cut if *off*. There's no down to it. They don't fall anywhere because of all that snow. You just take the chain saw and saw it off there. Then you measure up about sixteen inches a block of wood. You saw that off and take a head ax and knock it out of there. The tree drops down and you saw off another sixteen-inch block, and the tree drops down and you saw off another sixteen-inch block, knock it out and so on, until you get your load of wood. In the spring, why the limbs will be there somewhere. You can cut them up next summer and make them into wood for next year. I did that five or six loads, got plenty of wood down and split it up, piled it and put it in the shed there.

You know, you'd think that that would be real depressing to go through all that. But if you're smart and a good country person, why you'll figure out a use for everything. When spring come, everything thawed, all the water run down the hill and there laid all them tunnels. There laid all them tunnels and what are you going to do with all them tunnels?

I figured out that if I measured off about twenty or twenty-five feet on each one of them tunnels, and sawed it off with a chain saw, I could sell them to the highway department for culverts. I got right on the phone and I started calling. Next thing I knew I had quite a few orders. Even Mario Cuomo called me and wanted some state orders. I don't like to take a lot of state orders 'cause they're slow in paying. I would rather take the local orders but I took five or six of them state orders, too. I sold them to the highway departments for culverts.

When you're driving around this summer and you're seeing them workers digging out these old bridges, and doing all this road work and you see these big culverts there, you'll know they're some of my tunnels. You can tell 'em because they're kind of corrugated.

What I did is back them up to the side of the barn, I kept backing into them with the tractor, made them wrinkle so that they would hold more weight.

IF PEOPLE LIVED LIKE THAT TODAY, THEY'D ALL DIE

I remember when I was a kid, at night my father would let the fires go out. We had to cut wood with a crosscut saw. You didn't have no pipes to freeze or nothin', so you didn't care if it froze. You'd have about five or six of them big patchwork quilts on you. My mother'd take all the worn-out wool pants and all the wool frocks and everything and make them into patchwork quilts. They'd all sit around at night and sew these quilts together. They were heavy.

Well, when you got in bed at night, you'd have—not a linen sheet like we have now—but it was a sort of a flannel type sheet, and then on top of that you'd pile a bunch of these big old quilts. Whatever position you was gonna sleep in was the position you got in before you pulled the blankets up, because once you got them up there they were so heavy you couldn't turn over when you were a little kid. There you'd lay and pull the blankets right over your head and leave just a hole for just your nose and mouth to stick out to breathe. When you woke up in the morning there'd be icicles and frost all around that hole where you breathed out there all night.

You'd go downstairs, and there was a stick that laid there on the sink, a round club-type stick that had been whittled so it looked like a little billy club. You'd use that to break the ice in the water pail and then you could dip the water out. You'd get the stove going and, in no time at all, the whole house would be warm and everything would be back booming again. The next night the fire would go out and the next morning everything would be frozen, and all the whole nine yards all over again.

117

If people lived like that today, they'd all die. Nobody even cared or knew any different. It didn't mean a thing. You'd just get up in the morning and stir the fire up a little bit. See, them old houses, they weren't insulated like today people's houses are insulated. They weren't insulated.

So when it got 35-40 below at night, it dropped down to zero in the house and below sometimes. It was cold, but you weren't cold because you had all them blankets on you.

Today, times are hard and people are taking out their problems on everybody else. Nobody wants to help other folks; they just want to blame them. I believe people are responsible for their own actions.

But I grew up during World War II when the United States of America was something to be proud of and people all helped each other. We sacrificed and all worked together for the common cause to make the world a better place to live. Men went off to war and sacrificed their families and their lives while the women worked on the farms and in factories. Other women joined the different services and were nurses up near the front lines and others worked in government offices.

I had sisters that worked at the aluminum plant in Massena and rode the bus from Potsdam. I had one brother, Durwood, who got badly wounded in Belgium. My brother Richard went into the Merchant Marine. All my other brothers had hernias from loading pulpwood or working hard and the Army wouldn't take them.

I remember riding the roads with my mother and seeing the flags in the windows with one star on them for each child in the service. Pretty near every house had at least one. I'm sure it made parents feel better to know that they weren't the only ones suffering and missing their young ones.

Everyone helped the war effort, even us kids in school. We picked up cigarette packages, took the foil off them, and rolled them into balls. We took

118

the balls to school for when the government man came.

I remember we had the milkweed program. The mildweed pods were used by the Navy. They took the fluff out of those pods and filled the Mae West life jackets that were worn by our sailors and solidiers out on the water. A lot of us country kids would pick milkweed pods after school in late summer and fall. We took them to school by the bran sack full. "The Government Guy," we called him, would come to school and pick up those milkweed pods and he would leave stripes with the teacher. For so many bags we got a PFC stripe and for more we became a corporal and a sergeant and so on. We wore them on our sleeves and people knew we were in the Milkweed Patrol.

NOTES

In Snow Culverts, *Bill peoples travelling back-woods almanac and vaudeville yarns with local characters, descendants of the rural Yorkshire simpletons who get the best of London dandies and of New England's Jonathan Slick.*

Stories similar to "Mud Season" are told about travellers through swamps in this country and Europe. "Morris Rivers" is everybody's literal-minded favorite, the numbskull or [in the 1950's] the Little Moron.

Some of the best American tall tales and migratory jests are in 18th and 19th century travel accounts: Ethan Allen's A Narrative of Col. Ethan's Captivity; *John Jame's* Audubon's Ornithological Biography, Vol. I, *and William Byrd's* Histories of the Dividing Line Betwixt Virginia and North Carolina, *are full of lies, outrageous animals, and astonishing "natural wonders," as are the writings of Benjamin Franklin. Many of these stories were drawn from oral tradition. From the travel books, the tales began to be circulated in almanacs, from which they passed again into oral tradition!*

Bill's mind seems to work out stories within the traditional tall tale format. Growing up as he did, hearing so much traditional talk, Bill took in the structure of tall tales without really thinking about it. Today, I guess you'd have to say Bill can't help himself! "Snow Culverts" is Bill's own construction, turning on the category mistake, *the rigid application of the rules from one class to another, inappropriate, group or situation.*

In addition to the works mentioned earlier, it's worth rummaging around stores that sell used books for these titles: The American Imagination at Work,: Tall Tales and Folk Tales, *edited by Ben Clough [New York: Alfred A. Knopf, 1947];* Edith Cutting's Lore of an Adirondack County *[Ithaca, N.Y.: Cornell University Press, 1944]; and Richard*

Dorson's Jonathan Draws the Long Bow *[Cambridge, Mass.: Harvard University Press, 1946].*

Harold Thompson's Body, Boots, and Britches: Folktales, Ballads, and Speech from Country New York *[1939. Reprint, New York: Dover, 1967], is still in print. It is an anthology of folklore collected in the 1930's and 40's by Thompson's students at Albany Teachers' College. Reading it, we realize that rural New York was once as rich in oral lore as Southern Appalachia.*

* * * * *

It's important to Bill Smith that we experience his stories as a child would. The last story brings the war, the backdrop for everything else in those years, into focus. If we see those pre-nuclear days as our last era of national innocence, maybe these stories will remind us that innocence can be a sophisticated, comic choice in the face of the most terrible; that, like a child filling a bag with milkweed or a man spinning a good yarn, we must do what we can, from where we are, with what we have.

GOIN' TO CHURCH

When the stars are all a-glitter and the moon is shinin'
down,
And the air is seemin' cooler as the autumn rolls around,
Ah, it's nice to be in the mountains, just sittin' by a
stream,
Listenin' to the crickets and ponderin' your dreams.

You crawl into your bedroll and you breathe the cool,
fresh air,
And wake up from your slumber with the frost upon
your hair,
Wash your face in a cool clear stream—just takes your
breath away,
But it feels so refreshing as you're startin' out the day.

Have some bacon and some pancakes cooked on the
open fire.
Smell that coffee brewing! Now, there's something to
admire!
The sun comes peaking over the hill and the light
comes siftin' through.
You start to feelin' warmer and you can see that lovely
view.

And so you go out walkin' under crimson maple leaves,
And the yellow aspen's quakin' as it shivers in the
breeze.
The squirrels are gatherin' beechnuts and the deer
have all turned grey.
Birds have started flockin' and will soon be on their
way.

Don't you feel sort of reverent as you walk upon such
   sod?
For the the beauty of these mountains truly is a part of
   God.

Bill Smith

MORE ABOUT BILL SMITH

ARTICLES IN BOOKS

Adirondack Faces. Mathias Oppersdorff, 1990.
Exploring America's Back Country. National Geographic
  Special Edition,1979.
Adirondack Furniture. Craig Gilborn,1987

FEATURES IN MAGAZINES

New York Alive. Nov.–Dec. 1986.
Adirondack Life. 1986, 1989.
Prime of Life. Jan.–Feb. 1990.
Colonial Homes. April 1991.
National Geographic Traveller. April 1991.

STORIES IN COLLECTIONS

I Always Tell the Truth [Even If I Have to Lie to Do It].
  Vaughn Ward,ed., 1990.

AUDIO TAPES

Stories and Songs from the Featherbed
More Featherbed Stories
Tall Tales and Poems
Adirondack Memories
[featured in] *Sagamore Sampler #1 and #2*
[featured in] *An Adirondack Celebration*

VIDEO TAPES

Adirondack Images
Music from the Adirondacks

**BILL SMITH IS AVAILABLE FOR STORYTELLING
PERFORMANCES, BASKET AND ADIRONDACK
FURNITURE WORKSHOPS, CONFERENCES,
SCHOOLS, AND FESTIVALS**

RD 1
Colton, New York 13625
315–262–2436

ABOUT THE EDITOR

Vaughn Ramsey Ward, a displaced New Mexican with Southern Scots-Irish, Choctaw and Cherokee roots, has spent her adult life learning songs and stories from first-hand sources in the Adirondacks, Ireland and Scotland. A performing artist, teacher, folklorist, and writer, Ward has edited three previous collections of traditional stories for Bowman Books. In addition to her work as Folk Arts Specialist for the Lower Adirondack Regional Arts Council in Glens Falls, New York, Vaughn Ward works with her husband [composer and performing artist George Ward] in their presenting and production business, Blue Cat Concerns. The Wards live in Rexford, New York, on the old Erie Canal. Their mostly-grown sons, Nathaniel and Peter, still stop by regularly.